Terror from Within

Craig L'Esperance

Copyright © 2011 Craig L'Esperance
All rights reserved.

ISBN: 1-4611-1362-8
ISBN-13: 9781461113621

Dedication

This book is for all the hard working men and women who continue to put on the uniform every day, because they want to make a difference.

Acknowledgement

Thank you to everyone who assisted with the creation of this book, without your assistance this book would not have been possible.

Notice

This is a work of fiction. All names, characters, places, and incidents in this work are fictitious. Any resemblance to real people, living or dead is entirely coincidental.

Prologue

Monday, June 19th, Three Forks, Michigan

The large mahogany door behind the bailiff opened, and a middle-aged, white male, dressed in an orange jumpsuit, shuffled through the opening. His head was shaved, and everyone in the courtroom could see the ink from his many tattoos. He stood five feet, eight inches tall and weighed in at around 180 pounds. His tanned, muscular arms stuck out of his short sleeves.

A leather band encircled his waist, and his hands were secured to the band with handcuffs. His legs were shackled together, which made him slide his feet rather than walk with a normal gait.

The door shut behind him, but not before a rather large and unfit correctional officer waddled in behind the prisoner. The correctional officer was staring down at the brown clipboard he was holding in his hands. He was preoccupied with getting through the daily court call than keeping a close eye on the prisoner.

The prisoner approached the bench and joined the public defender, who had already called his case before the Honorable Judge Brown.

The bailiff sat down in his chair, at the end of the bench. He began reading his book, as he normally did during his courtroom security duties. His officer safety skills were lacking, but this did not seem to worry anyone. The bailiff happened to be the only person in the courtroom with a firearm as he was assigned to protect the judge and the citizens who appeared in the courtroom.

Judge Brown glanced down to look over the case before him. This case had already been continued several times on the state's attorney's motion, and it was obvious to the judge that the state was stalling this case to allow further time for the completion of the investigation.

As Judge Brown was reviewing the status of the case, the prisoner suddenly fell to the ground and rolled into a ball. He moaned as if he was in some sort of pain.

To the twenty or so people in the courtroom, it appeared as though the prisoner was having a heart attack.

All eyes watched the prisoner, except for four subjects who were sitting in separate areas of the courtroom. They quickly stood up and walked to the center aisle. Two of them were dressed in long, dark business overcoats. The second two were wearing bulky tan jackets.

Before the bailiff could react to what was unfolding in front of him, one of the subjects pulled out an assault rifle and pointed it at the bailiff.

"Don't anyone move or make a sound," the subject yelled as a few muffled cries could be heard in the witness benches. "Anyone who attempts to make a phone call or tries to be a hero will be shot." To add emphasis to his demands, he quickly waived the gun over the crowd before settling his sights back on the bailiff.

The bailiff didn't even have a chance to raise his gun. His mind began spinning, as he quickly thought about his predicament. He had been a police officer for twenty-eight years before retiring from general police work and transitioning into a full-time position as a court security officer. He had never once come upon anything of this magnitude in his entire career.

The second subject pulled out an assault rifle as well and retreated towards the back of the courtroom, standing off to the side of the doorway. He was wearing a dark-blue baseball cap and it was pulled down tightly over his eyes.

The third and fourth subjects rushed towards the fallen prisoner. One of them pulled a handcuff key out of his pocket and unlocked the prisoner's shackles.

By this time, the people seated in the courtroom had all ducked below the benches and were completely silent.

Just as the prisoner was un-handcuffed, the door at the back of the courtroom opened and a young police officer walked through the doorway. His hand immediately reached for his gun as the second subject raised his assault rifle and fired two .223 rounds into the forehead of the officer. The officer slumped against the wall and slowly fell sideways as he hit the ground. A streak of blood arched along the wall from where the police officer had struck it, to where he lay on the floor.

The third subject reached under his jacket and pulled out a black semi-automatic handgun. He grabbed the prisoner's arm, and they ran towards the back of the courtroom.

The first subject who still had his assault rifle trained on the bailiff quickly walked backwards as he kept his rifle aimed at the bailiff.

The bailiff was quickly trying to decide what to do; his Colt .357 wheel gun was no match against several high-powered rifles. He would only be able to get off six rounds before having to reload, and it was at that point that he'd be riddled with bullets from these maniacs. He chose to stand quietly and watch as all five subjects disappeared out the far courtroom door.

Chapter 1
Detroit, Michigan

Two weeks after Sam Jenson's proposal, Robert Whitlock met him at the Legend. It was Saturday morning when they got into Sam's Escalade and drove east on I-96 towards downtown Detroit. Sam had arranged to travel with Robert into Detroit so they could meet with one of his connections. Their plan was to stop at the MGM Grand Casino in Detroit for a quick lunch and then meet up with his contact at a small liquor store on the south side of the city.

The MGM Grand Detroit Casino was built in July of 1999 in an attempt to bring added revenue to the city. The casino added about 1000 jobs to Detroit, in an area where the Big Three automakers were still the main employers in the now stumbling local economy.

Not far from the casino was Comerica Park, home of the Detroit Tigers. Robert had watched many games at the old Tiger Stadium, located at the corner Michigan and Trumbull. It was disappointing to see the lack of a central businesses district downtown, the kind that would attract people in larger cities like New York or Chicago.

Detroit was known for its raucous celebrations after a major sports team won a championship. After the Detroit Tigers won the World Series championship in 1984, the revelers in the street went wild, torching cars and buildings and overturning police cars.

But today wasn't about the Tigers or the history of Detroit. Robert was about to be one step closer to starting his new job with Sam.

They arrived at the casino at 11:26 a.m. and found a parking spot relatively close to the entrance. They grabbed some lunch and tried their luck at a few slot machines before leaving and heading towards the liquor store. The store didn't open until 1 p.m. on Saturdays because the owner couldn't find any reliable help to open the store any earlier.

As they drove through the city, Robert viewed so many burned-out and boarded-up buildings that he lost count. Gang graffiti tagged everything within reach, including viaducts and billboards.

The liquor store was on the southeast corner of Nineteenth and Industrial. It was a non-descript, two-story block building and it appeared to be the only occupied building within eyesight. Several neon signs flashed through the barred windows. This wasn't exactly the place you wanted to be during the daytime, let alone when it got dark.

According to FBI statistics, Detroit had been ranked in the top five for violent crimes for any city in the country for several years running. In 2006 alone, there were over 400 homicides in the city of Detroit.

Sam pulled out his cell phone and called the owner of the liquor store, Rafael Guzman. Guzman instructed him to pull around to the north side of the building so they could park inside of the garage.

Terror from Within

Guzman once told Sam that if he left his vehicle parked out on the street while he went inside the store, it would most likely be gone when he returned. He told Sam that if the car wasn't stolen, the rims and anything valuable from the inside would be missing.

Sam had met Guzman several years back while they were both in the Ryan Correctional Facility. Sam had been serving time for burglary and was housed in the same pod as Guzman, who was serving time for fraud and money laundering.

Guzman was well known in certain circles for his ability to produce and distribute high-quality fictitious driver's licenses and false vehicle registrations. Guzman still had connections from the days when he worked for the Michigan Secretary of State's Office, where he provided citizens with their driver's licenses, vehicle registrations, and titles. His access to the statewide database allowed him to see when anyone's driver's license or license plates were ran by a law enforcement official.

They pulled into the garage and parked as the garage door rattled closed behind them. Guzman came out through a small door on the far side of the garage. He was only five-foot-six-inches tall but weighed at least 300 pounds. He had a shaved head and a small goatee that stopped just below his second chin. He was wearing an oversized Detroit Lions #20 Barry Sanders jersey with a pair of loose-fitting gray sweatpants. A pair of shining-white gym shoes completed his outfit. A big gold chain hung around his neck and swayed from side to side as he approached them. Guzman extended his arms and gave Sam a great big hug.

"Sammy, it's great to see you again," Guzman said. "It's been too long, my friend."

"This is my friend, Robert," Sam added as he turned to introduce him.

Robert extended his right hand and firmly shook Guzman's massive hand.

"I've heard all about you, and it's a pleasure to be able to put a name to a face," Robert exclaimed.

"Let's go up to my office, and we can talk. Either of you want something to drink?"

They both nodded and asked for a cold Miller Lite.

Guzman led them down a dark hallway where a single light bulb was dangling precariously from the ceiling. They ducked under the light bulb and started up the steel-grated staircase.

Once they reached the second floor, it seemed as though they were in another building. The upstairs had been converted into the ultimate bachelor pad. Several flat-screen televisions were mounted on the walls. Two black-leather couches faced a sixty-inch LCD television. A large bar was built into the corner and housed several refrigerators. The refrigerators were loaded with every kind of beverage one could think of. The walls in the room were covered in all types of sports memorabilia, beer signs, and several posters of the Dallas Cowboys cheerleaders. Robert could see a bathroom off to the right and what appeared to be an office to the left. Guzman grabbed several beers out of the refrigerator, and they walked into the office.

They sat down on the leather executive chairs that surrounded a light-colored maple desk.

Terror from Within

"What can I do for you guys today?" Guzman said as he looked over at them.

"Well, Robert recently purchased a nineteen ninety-nine Ford panel van and he needs new registration for it. He also needs a new driver's license. I wanted to see if you could help us out."

Guzman pulled a black leather binder out from under a slot in his desk. He opened the binder and thumbed through several pages before landing on the one he needed.

"Sammy, you've always taken good care of me, so I will cut you a deal from my normal price. The registration will run you two hundred fifty and the driver's license will run three hundred fifty."

"What is your turnaround time for these items to be completed?" Sam asked.

"Give me until next weekend, and everything will be taken care of. I need to take a photo of Robert and get the vehicle identification number for the van."

Robert pulled a stack of paperwork from a manila envelope he was carrying. He slid the van's title over to Guzman.

"I haven't signed the title because I wanted to wait until I received the new driver's license to complete the buyer's information," Robert added.

Guzman took the title for the van and ran it through his scanner. He handed the title back to Robert.

"If you could stand up against that wall," Guzman said, pointing to the wall next to his desk. "I'll snap a few photos, and we'll be all set."

Robert stood up from his chair and set his beer down on a coaster that was on Guzman's desk. He stood with his back to the wall, and Guzman took several photos of him using a digital camera.

"Anything else I can do for you guys?" Guzman asked as he began downloading the photos onto his computer.

Sam pulled a wad of cash out of his pocket and thumbed through it before tossing six crisp one hundred dollar bills on the desk.

"No, I think that's it," Sam added, finishing the last sip of his beer. "I'd really like to hang out for a while, but we've got some more stuff we need to do today."

"Thanks again; we really appreciate it," Robert said as he tossed his beer can into the recycle bin.

"Anytime you guys need anything, you know where to find me," Guzman added, sliding the cash into his pocket.

Sam and Robert left Guzman's store and traveled back to Belcher. Earlier in the week, Robert had searched several Internet classified ads and he was able to locate a used ladder rack for the top of the van. The ladder rack would help him blend into his new position. They met with the seller and were able to buy the ladder rack with cash. They placed it into the back of Sam's SUV and they left the elderly gentleman's house.

They made a trip to the local Radio Shack store and purchased a police scanner. Robert would have to install the scanner under the dash of the van because having police scanners inside a vehicle is illegal and he didn't want to raise any suspicions during their new jobs.

Terror from Within

A stop off at the local hardware store, and they were able purchase a tool pouch, pry bar, bolt cutters, saw, blue coveralls, and mechanics work gloves. The only thing missing for their new uniforms would be patches and a name tag. Robert knew right where to go when it came to getting those items.

The local cable company's main facility was located on the west side of Belcher. Robert drove to the facility after dark and was able to rummage through the dumpster unnoticed. He came away with several worn-out uniforms with the patches and names still intact. He returned to the motel and worked configuring the newly obtained uniforms.

Sam had already obtained a storage unit on the west side of Belcher to store the van and equipment. This storage facility was built in the seventies and lacked many of today's security features. The facility didn't have any security cameras or code to enter the facility. It was in a relatively remote location and would allow for easy exit and entrance without being constantly monitored by anyone. He signed the lease using his false identification and paid cash for a year's worth of rent.

Chapter 2
Belcher, Michigan

Within two weeks, Sam had picked out their first target. In the meantime, Robert had obtained the documents from Guzman and was able to get the new license plates installed on the van.

Their first burglary happened to be at the residence of a prominent local business owner, Tim Osborn. The Osborns owned a furniture store and numerous apartment buildings in the Humble County area. Robert had used several Internet resources to locate Tim's address on Crabapple Lane on the east side of Belcher. The Crabapple subdivision consisted of isolated estates covered with maple and pine trees. This area was well known for its northern Michigan appeal while still being close to the metro Detroit area. The problem with living in this type of subdivision was it became a perfect target for Sam's newly hatched plan.

Sam and Robert met at the Legend at 9:15 a.m. on Tuesday morning. Through Sam's connections, he knew the local lawn maintenance company, which was used by everyone in the subdivision, wouldn't be in the area on Tuesdays. This would offer the best chance at going up to the house without anyone seeing.

It wouldn't be abnormal for cable workers to be present in the area during normal business hours, performing line maintenance. With the boom of the dot com era, nearly everyone in the area had the Internet, and this played right into their game plan.

They had used Google Maps for research prior to attempting this job. Its interactive street and satellite view allowed them to examine the property without actually driving by the house and risking the chance of being spotted, or having a nosy neighbor call the police. As Robert eased the van into the driveway, he knew they couldn't be seen from the house until they reached the second bend in the driveway.

Once onto the driveway, Sam jumped out of the van and quickly placed a sensor in the grass on one side of the driveway and a reflector directly opposite the sensor on the other side of the driveway. This driveway alarm, which Sam had purchased from an online retailer, was the only chance they had of leaving the residence in the event the homeowner arrived home while they were at work.

As the asphalt driveway slowly moved under them, Robert couldn't help but try to stay calm. Their preplanning was excellent, but there were always variables that were out of their control. Sam had briefed Robert on the possibility that the Osborns could have an alarm system; they could have stayed home for the day or even have a dog. More importantly, they could be in the residence when someone came home, and that would present more problems.

As the van rounded the second bend in the driveway, Robert watched for but didn't see any signs of activity at the house. He parked near the garage, and they exited the van. They were both dressed in a dark blue coveralls, white hard hats, and brown work boots; a tool pouch hung from their waists. A black pair of tight-fitting mechanic's gloves would allow them to quickly perform their tasks and not leave any fingerprints. Robert was impressed with the level of planning Sam had completed prior to attempting this job.

Sam stayed near the van and monitored his portable police scanner via a small ear piece. If there were any signs of trouble, he would make contact with Robert via his small portable radio.

Robert calmly walked along the side of the garage and up the walkway. The front walkway was made of brick and was surrounded by flower gardens that were still several months from being in full bloom. At the end of the walkway, three steps rose up to the all-brick porch. His plan was simple; if someone answered the door, he would advise the homeowner he was in the area performing line maintenance and wanted to make sure they weren't having any cable issues. If nobody answered the door after several minutes, he would enter the residence through the walkout basement.

Robert grabbed a hold of the lion-shaped knocker and struck it on the door several times. He paused for a minute and didn't hear any movement from inside of the house. After knocking several more times and ringing the doorbell, his nerves eased a bit. Robert still hadn't heard any movement from inside of the house. He left the front porch and walked back towards the garage. As he passed the van, he couldn't help but notice a small blue yard sign sticking ominously out of the flower bed. The sign read: "This house is protected by an electronic monitoring system." This sign in itself was enough for Robert's palms to become moist and his heart to skip a beat. A single bead of sweat ran down the left side of his forehead. If there were, in fact, an alarm, he would most likely hear it and be able to leave the area prior to the arrival of the police. Sam had previously told Robert that with all the recent funding cuts, there was a good chance it would take a while for an officer to respond to the alarm.

Robert continued around the side of the garage and walked down the stamped concrete walkway towards the back of the house.

The back of the home rose above the ground with grand distinction. With the two stories and full basement, the house looked like a mansion. It overlooked an in-ground swimming pool and a backyard that was professionally landscaped with numerous bushes and flowers. A patio area contained a grill and several pieces of outdoor furniture. A dense line of pine trees surrounded the backyard and offered a tranquil up-north style setting.

Robert snapped his attention to the back of the house. The sun wasn't yet shining into the backyard, which allowed Robert to see in most of the big picture windows. He didn't notice any movement on the first or second floor. The shades on the fully finished basement windows were wide open and offered an unobstructed view inside.

Robert reached the sliding glass door that led into the basement. Pausing for a second, he pressed a button on the two-way radio. "How are we lookin'?"

There was a brief pause, and then Sam's voice came into his earpiece. "We're home free."

Robert slowly turned the knob on the sliding glass door and, as he figured, it was locked. After trying several of the basement windows, he returned to the door. Fortunately, the homeowners didn't have a deadbolt lock on this door. He retrieved a pry bar from his tool pouch and began working on the lock side of the door. Within seconds, Robert had pried open the door and was inside the basement.

Chapter 3
Three Forks, Michigan

Blake arrived at work at 8:53 a.m. on Tuesday morning with a massive headache. He had been out all night processing the scene of an armed robbery at a twenty-four hour gas station on the west side of Three Forks. Someone had entered the store at 1:12 a.m. and proceeded to rob the clerk at gunpoint. Blake had been called in to process the scene for evidence a short time after responding deputies had arrived. The sheriff's office K-9 Rocky was called to start a track on the fleeing robbery suspect. Blake arrived at the gas station and immediately viewed the surveillance video to gather as much evidence as he could. The suspect was dressed in blue jeans, a hooded sweatshirt, and a light-colored baseball hat. The subject had brandished a chrome handgun and fled the area with a small amount of cash. Blake interviewed the clerk to gather more details of the incident. Because of the time of the burglary, there were not any other witnesses. The K-9 tracked the suspect northbound from the business and into the parking lot of an adjacent industrial building. The suspect's scent disappeared in that area, which indicated the suspect most likely fled the area in a vehicle.

Blake was on scene until almost 4:30 a.m. and had returned to the sheriff's office afterwards to secure the evidence he had gathered into a locker. When he returned home, he was able to get about an hour of sleep before his alarm sounded for his regular shift. The lack of sleep was part of the job, and Blake knew this when he put in to be transferred into the detective bureau. This still didn't help lessen the effects of his pounding headache, which seemed to start at the back of his eyes and shoot straight to the back of his head.

The detective bureau had recently moved into the new addition at the sheriff's office, and everyone was pleased with the upgrade. They had previously worked in a single office that didn't have separate cubicles. The telephone noise on any given day was almost unbearable. The ventilation system had failed miserably years ago, and it left their back corner windowless office at a constant temperature of sixty degrees. It wasn't uncommon for everyone to have a sweatshirt hanging on the metal coat rack even in the summer months.

Blake attended roll call and caught everyone up to speed on the early morning robbery. With only five detectives on staff, their division was barely able to keep its head above water. The recent talks about layoffs would only hamper their ability to handle the current caseload. This would lead to shorter times between each detective being on call.

Blake worked the entire day following up on the gas station robbery. He had to cancel several previously scheduled appointments so he could follow up on the leads he had for the robbery. He continued to receive telephone calls throughout the day from victims of other cases he was handling, inquiring as to the status of their cases. Blake had to politely tell them he was doing the best he

Terror from Within

could under the current circumstances and that he would keep them updated with any new developments. Blake had to educate some of the victims on how the investigation process worked, and that his caseload was pretty heavy. He empathized with the victims, but he could only do so much with some of the cases he was assigned. He constantly had to prioritize, and some people didn't understand how their case could be sitting idle on his desk. Crimes against people were the first to be investigated, and crimes against property became secondary on his list of priorities.

It was 5:15 p.m. and Blake began winding down the robbery investigation for the day. He heard the telephone ring in the secretary's office, and the call was forwarded to Detective Sergeant McGuire.

A few minutes later, McGuire entered Blake's office. "I need you to head over to a residence in Belcher to process a burglary scene. The homeowner is a well-known Belcher businessman and a good friend of the sheriff. Their house was burglarized sometime earlier today when they were at work. One of our deputies is on scene and is requesting a detective respond to the scene to do the processing." McGuire didn't have any further details on the case, as he was on his way out of his office when his phone rang.

Sergeant McGuire had worked as a detective prior to his promotion and knew all too well what it felt like to have plans interrupted because of a call out.

Since they didn't have anyone working the afternoon shift, and Blake was currently on call, the detective sergeant didn't have any choice on whom to assign this case to.

"I'm sorry to throw this into your lap," Sergeant McGuire added as he was leaving Blake's office.

"I'll finish this follow-up investigation tomorrow," Blake said as he saved his report and started shutting down his computer. He threw a quick glance at McGuire as he turned to gather his portable radio. "I'll shoot you an e-mail after I'm done processing the scene to keep you updated on the details of this burglary."

Sergeant McGuire had no worries about Blake's ability to handle a case and make sure all the leads were followed up. "I'll see you in the morning," he said as he turned and walked down the hallway.

"See ya in the morning."

Blake knew better than to make excuses for why he needed to be home for dinner this evening. He gathered his laptop computer and portable radio, and left the office a few minutes later.

He was originally scheduled to be off work at 5:00 p.m. and was planning on being home for dinner because Maria's parents were coming over. She was making lasagna, which happened to be his favorite meal, and he hadn't had a chance to visit with his in-laws in several months.

Blake unlocked the door to his unmarked squad car and placed his belongings on the front passenger seat. He shut the door and was soon headed towards Belcher to process the scene of the burglary. He pulled his cell phone out of his pocket and held down speed dial number two, and his phone began ringing.

"Hello, dear," Blake said as he tried not to sound disappointed. "Are your parents there yet?"

"No, I'm sure they'll be here any minute." Maria added, "Are you just leaving work?"

"Yea, but unfortunately I have to run out to Belcher and process the scene of a burglary. Patrol doesn't have an evidence technician working; the victim is friends with the sheriff."

Blake could hear an exhausted sigh at the other end of the phone. "These kids have been absolutely terrible today, and this house is a disaster. I was counting on you coming home before my parents arrived, so you could help me clean up. It figures you always get called out whenever we make any sort of family plans."

"Honey, I'm sorry about this. I wish I didn't have to head over there, either, and you know that." Blake knew this wasn't going to help the matter, and he really hated when he had to miss family functions because of work. "I'll call you when I'm on the way home and hopefully I can make it before your parents leave."

Maria was frustrated, and Blake could sense the tension through the phone line. He knew it wasn't easy for her to juggle a full-time job along with taking care of their children when Blake was called into work. He had watched the kids in the past while Maria was at work and it wasn't easy taking care of them all day long. Their children were too young and weren't independent, and this meant Blake had to make breakfast, clean up after breakfast, brush their teeth, and get them changed into their clothes for the day. He changed soiled diapers and washed clothes. And usually by the end of the day, Blake was completely worn out. He was certain that he couldn't be paid enough to be a stay-at-home parent.

The conversation with Maria only helped fuel his already throbbing headache. Maria had known his career path prior to marrying him but she still found a reason to complain about his work.

This was the one downfall of being a detective versus being a patrol deputy. When Blake was on patrol, he could do his job and go home at the end of his shift, not having to worry about getting called out. There was rarely ever an incident that required him to follow-up on a case for several days. Now, being on call for almost two full weeks a month was taking a toll on him. His cases were always on his mind, and if he happened to take a day off, there wasn't anyone there to keep working on his cases. They all sat on his desk, and new cases continued piling up, as if they were going to magically solve themselves.

Blake arrived at the Osborn residence at 5:51 p.m. The initial responding deputy filled him in on the details of this incident. Mr. Osborn had left the residence around 8:15 a.m. to go to work and had forgotten to set the alarm system. His wife was out of town for work, and nobody else was home during the day. Mr. Osborn arrived home at 4:45 p.m. to find his house had been ransacked.

Blake spoke with Mr. Osborn briefly as he surveyed the area in and around the residence. As with the majority of his crime scenes, he quickly learned that Mr. Osborn was a CSI fanatic. Blake kind of enjoyed dispelling most of the things that happened on that particular television show.

Blake took photos of the scene using his department-issued point-and-shoot digital camera. It didn't take long for Mr. Osborn to realize that Blake didn't have all of the

Terror from Within

fancy CSI gadgets that would have the case solved within the hour.

Blake documented that the rear door had been pried open with some sort of pry bar or large screwdriver. He took tool impressions from the door, using a two-part compound that adhered to the doorframe and created a rubberized mold of the damage. This mold would be sent to the crime lab for analysis. Blake dusted many areas of the residence for fingerprints and was able to lift several latent fingerprints. Blake took elimination fingerprints from Mr. Osborn, so the crime lab could compare them to the latent fingerprints recovered at the scene. Blake told Mr. Osborn he would meet with Mrs. Osborn to take her fingerprints once she returned from her trip.

Mr. Osborn wasn't able to narrow down the timeframe of the burglary because the alarm system wasn't activated. Blake canvassed several nearby residences, and nobody had seen or heard anything suspicious in the area.

Blake left the residence at 7:21 p.m. and drove back to the sheriff's office. He completed an evidence report form and then placed the items he had collected into a secure evidence locker.

It was 8:26 p.m. by the time Blake left the sheriff's office and got into his car to drive home. It was dark outside, and rising gas prices were a great recipe for light traffic.

The in-law's car was no longer in the driveway as Blake pulled into the garage and shut the door behind him. Blake hoped that Maria was over the fact that he had to miss dinner.

He walked into the mudroom and could hear the children upstairs brushing their teeth. He took his shoes off and hung his coat up on the hook.

Maria came downstairs and saw that he had arrived home.

"Hi, dear," she said as she began picking up the toys in the adjoining living room.

"Hi, sorry I had to miss dinner. How are your parents doing?"

"They're doing well. They haven't seen you in a while, so they were disappointed that you had to work late."

"I know. I hope you apologized for me. I can't predict when someone's going to commit a crime," Blake added, half jokingly.

"Dinner is in the fridge; you'll have to heat it up in the microwave. The kids are in bed and waiting for you to say good night to them."

Blake gave Maria a kiss and hurried upstairs to give the kids a kiss goodnight. He said good night to the children and apologized for missing dinner with their grandparents, but the kids didn't seem to mind.

After tucking them into bed and seeing how their days went, Blake returned downstairs and heated up the rest of the lasagna. He later climbed into bed and was asleep before his head hit the pillow.

Chapter 4

Blake returned to the sheriff's office on Wednesday morning, just in time to attend the morning roll call.

After roll call, he checked his voice-mail and then worked on generating leads for the burglary to the Osborns' residence. Blake called the local Department of Corrections parole office and spoke with the officer for the Humble County area.

Blake filled the parole officer in on the burglary case and asked to get a copy of the parolees from the county. The parole agent informed him that their commander instructed they were no longer allowed to distribute the list of parolees to local police agencies. There were too many recent instances in the city where the police were using the parole officers as a stepping stone to search a residence for evidence of the crimes where a parolee was suspected.

This new mandate didn't surprise Blake. He realized that the main concern for the DOC parole office was to try to rehabilitate as many offenders as they could without putting them back into prison. This was a fine motto to stand by, right up to the point where the parolees were still committing crimes and, in essence, being protected by their parole agent from re-arrest.

So, in the case of this recent burglary, it would be beneficial for Blake to have a copy of the parole list and to see who was on parole for this type of burglary. This would at least give him some direction prior to the crime laboratory results coming back. As it occurred, in most cases, parolees would usually keep reoffending and never be rehabilitated like the court system would like to think they were.

Blake ended his phone call with the DOC parole agent and checked his e-mails. There was an e-mail from the sheriff stating that—effective immediately—the department would be issuing pink slips to twelve deputies. With the new restructuring, two of the least senior detectives were going to be sent back to road patrol. His mind wandered to the families of those deputies who were going to be laid off. It wasn't going to be the "retired on duty" slackers who would be laid off because the union provided them with protection. It was going to be the deputies who were worthless and a liability to the department. Based upon seniority, the layoffs were going to affect the least senior deputies first. To Blake, this was the biggest problem with being part of the union. It laid blanket protection over the deputies and guaranteed the "slugs" job security.

This meant the department had spent nearly $100,000 to train and equip each one of these deputies, and now they were going to be laid off. With the recent hiring blitzes in larger cities, like the Las Vegas Metro Police and Los Angeles Police Department, there was a good chance that the sheriff's department had trained these deputies, and they would be leaving the area to find other employment.

The e-mail contained no mention of an early buyout for the deputies who were close to retirement. To Blake, this option seemed to make the most sense, as they took up a huge chunk of the payroll and, for the most part, did the least amount of work.

With his seniority in the detective bureau, Blake would be able to stay in the bureau and would become the least senior detective. The increased caseload was sure to take its toll on the positive closure of cases.

Sergeant McGuire had a job to do, and it consisted of assigning all the new cases to the detectives for follow-up investigation. He had a bottom line to look out for, and that was making sure the cases were being handled properly and to the fullest extent possible. He normally would read all of the reports to make sure the detectives followed up on any potential leads available in the cases.

Blake knew his caseload was going to increase significantly within the first few weeks. With a new average of fifty cases open at one time, it was quickly becoming impossible to work each case effectively before the witnesses and active leads became stale.

Chapter 5
Belcher, MI

The burglary at the Osborns' had yielded unprecedented results. Two flat-screen televisions, jewelry, power tools, and two Blu-ray DVD players were taken. The local pawnshops and cash for gold stores enabled Robert to easily get rid of these items with no questions asked. He dropped off the electronics and power tools at a pawnshop on the south side of Three Forks and was paid $417 for these items. They were able to pawn these items without even being requested to show any form of identification, which kept Robert's mind at ease. It wasn't that he was worried about his fraudulent identification being compromised, he just didn't want to leave it to chance.

After pawning the stolen items, they drove the van over to the rural storage facility, which was deserted as usual. They rarely ran into anyone else coming or going, and it was the main reason why Sam had picked this location to store the van. Robert pulled up to the storage unit and parked the van. Sam climbed out of the passenger seat, opened up the garage door, and backed his Cadillac Escalade out of the garage.

Robert pulled the van into the garage, and Sam shut the door behind them. They quickly changed out of their matching blue jumpsuits and into clean clothes. The blue jumpsuits were hung on the small coat rack located at the rear of the storage unit. The storage unit wasn't the cleanest place, as there were numerous oily rags strewn around the room from when Robert changed the oil in the van. Cob webs filled the corners, and several dimly lit lights cast a glow down from above. They took one look around to make sure they weren't forgetting anything before leaving out the service door and locking it behind them. Sam jumped into his Cadillac, Robert hopped into the passenger seat, and they left the area.

ಇ⊷ಆ

Robert sat down at their normal booth at the Legend and flipped open his pre-paid cell phone, dialing a number from memory.

"Yea," was the only response that Sam gave him.

"I'm at work right now," Robert whispered into the phone.

With that statement, the line went dead. They had developed several terms that would allow them to effectively communicate and avoid any eavesdropping. Sam was excellent at making sure that every base was covered when it came to planning their new jobs.

Sam had previously explained the reasons for the pre-paid cell phones. If they paid cash for these phones, there would be no contracts to pay and no credit checks. He could change phones and numbers as frequently as needed, and he would be able to stay one step ahead of any law enforcement investigations. Sam had explained the process for which the cops had to go through to obtain these records. It involved many subpoenas and grand juries that, in turn, became tough to prove when one individual couldn't be tied to a particular cell phone. Sam had actually purchased Robert's first cell phone from a local big box retailer. The features were actually surprisingly good and included three-way calling, voice-mail, and text/picture messaging capabilities. Communication was Sam's top priority and he wanted to make sure Robert had the best local coverage.

Robert's thoughts turned to his family as he ordered another beer; he hadn't seen his kids in over a month. It was killing him that his wife wasn't willing to work with him on his personal problems.

For the time being, he decided to continue with this new job, and when the economy got better, he promised himself that he would find a legitimate job and return to being a normal, productive member of society. Although he couldn't complain because he had only worked several hours and his cut would be more than $300. Sam had agreed to give Robert a majority of the proceeds because he had other sources of income. Robert was still forced to make payments on the mortgage for the house that he was no longer living in. Sam had made it clear that their boundaries would have to expand beyond Humble County to become successful in their new business venture.

Sam arrived at the Legend a half hour later. He walked directly to the booth and slid into the seat across from Robert.

"You look like shit," Sam said as he leaned over and placed a coaster in front of him and grabbed a menu.

Sam hadn't eaten all day and was in the mood for some greasy bar food.

"Thanks," Robert replied gruffly as he resumed the death stare at the bottle he was holding in his hand.

"I need to fill you in on a job that I have drummed up for tonight," Sam added, nonchalantly.

A blonde waitress arrived as Sam was finishing his sentence.

"What can I get for you tonight, hon?" She asked as she batted her long eyelashes at Sam.

"I'll have a bacon cheeseburger with American cheese with a basket of steak fries."

"What would you like to drink?"

"I'll take a Miller Lite."

Robert figured Sam wouldn't get too plastered, as he would be most likely driving to the new job tonight. Robert didn't want to be driving because he already had a slight buzz going.

The waitress scooped up the menu and disappeared.

"John will be here in a little bit. I'll fill you in on the way over to the job site."

Robert's son had played on the same baseball team as John Gibson's son for many years, and they had become friends over the years before losing contact with each other.

Sam's cheeseburger arrived, and he quickly consumed it. He chased it down with the last swig of his beer just as his cell phone rang.

"Go ahead."

Sam paused for a second as he listened to the person on the other end of the line. Then he flipped his phone shut and clipped it back on his belt.

"John said he'll be here in a minute, and he'll meet us outside by my truck."

Sam raised his right arm and flagged the waitress down.

Terror from Within

"We gotta run; can we get our tab?"

She hurried off and returned a minute later with the bill. Sam pulled out a wad of cash and threw some money on the table.

"Your beer's on me tonight; let's get rolling."

Robert left the table and stopped in the restroom to relieve himself.

John pulled into the parking lot just as Robert exited the Legend and parked next to Sam's black Escalade.

With the temperature hovering right around fifty degrees, Robert couldn't help but think of what was to come, as spring would eventually turn into summer. Their jobs were sure to increase and the recent foreclosure statement he had received would become an afterthought. He needed to keep the mortgage afloat to have a chance at recovering some of the market's losses, once the divorce situation was rectified.

John exited his truck and locked the doors. Sam was already sitting in the driver's seat of his Cadillac, and John got into the front passenger seat. Robert took the back seat behind John and shut the door behind them.

Sam explained where their job site was going to be and Sam's Escalade would fit into the environment with no problem.

The Clearwater area was well known for its million-dollar mansions and prestigious private Catholic schools. The area schools annually produce top honor students along with state championship sports teams. These state championships usually caused quite the debate over Catholic schools having their own league versus playing in the public school leagues. The families who reside in Clearwater are mostly executives, doctors, lawyers, judges, and even some local celebrities.

Sam had eased his Escalade onto Interstate 96 and headed east towards Detroit. They went from one of the fastest-growing counties in the country to the vast sprawling areas of suburban metro Detroit. They continued in near silence as they exited off Interstate 96, merged onto Interstate 696 east, and continued towards Clearwater.

The traffic was light at this time of night, and the lack of any springtime construction on the interstate made the trip go by a little faster. Michigan always had massive road construction projects that progressed throughout three out of the four seasons of the year. Winter was the only time this construction ceased, but the constant freezing and thawing caused massive potholes that would wreak havoc on traveling motorist.

They continued east on Interstate 696 before turning to head south on Interstate 94.

Sam filled Robert and John in on his game plan for this evening's job. The yacht club appeared to be an easy hit compared to some of the recent jobs they had performed. The risk of people being in the area was relatively low, due to the time of year. With three people in on this job, it would be a little easier to keep an eye out for anything that could possibly ruin their plans.

Sam pulled off Interstate 94 at the Vernier Road exit and headed east. Sam handed them maps of the area surrounding the yacht club; it was situated on Lake St. Clair and there were numerous exits/entrances to the area. An aerial view of the area showed no signs of any security fence or gated entrance.

Terror from Within

Sam explained how he had driven to the area earlier in the week to get a better idea as to the exact layout. Sam said the security firm that usually patrolled the area had yet to start patrolling for the new year. Since most of the boats were still waiting in storage, the large parking lot would be packed with everything from sailboats to massive cabin cruisers, all covered with blue shrink-wrap. With the security company not yet patrolling the area, the Clearwater Police Department would be the first to respond to any signs of trouble.

As they pulled into the entrance, Robert saw the sign welcoming them to the Clearwater Yacht Club. He could see the yacht club was off to the right. It was 11:07 p.m. on his watch, and this meant that the Clearwater Police would probably be right in the middle of a shift change.

Sam dialed up the police department's non-emergency telephone number. He blocked his own number so the dispatcher wasn't able to trace the number or location. He told the dispatcher that a fight was in progress at a tavern on the south side of town. This would allow them time to complete the mission prior to the arrival of the local black and white.

The Clearwater Yacht Club happened to be one of the most prestigious yacht clubs, not only in Michigan, but in the nation. It was highly rated for its top-notch customer service and amenities. It boasted several indoor tennis courts, an Olympic-sized pool, large exercise room, locker rooms complete with saunas and hot tubs, and a lounge with several flat-screen televisions. The club hosted many events throughout the year, including sailing competitions and large conferences. People came from all over the world to enjoy the food that was prepared by a world-famous chef. The initial membership buy-in was $50,000, and the monthly dues ran right around $1500. The clientele consisted of the ultra rich, and the amenities spoke for themselves.

The main building was three stories of native New England stone and marble. The entire back portion contained massive windows that overlooked the marina. Beyond the marina was Lake St. Clair, which leads south to the St. Clair River, which then dumps into Lake Erie. From there, you could travel all the way to the Atlantic Ocean.

The loading docks were on the north side of the yacht club and were obscured by several tall rows of neatly planted pine trees. Sam parked his Escalade near a dumpster just north of the loading docks. If the place had video surveillance cameras, they surely wouldn't pick up his vehicle from where it was parked. They all exited the car and gently pushed the doors shut. They had already donned black 5.11 tactical gloves and were wearing baseball hats. Their cell phones were left on vibrate, and each carried a small hand-held radio stuffed in their back pockets. They all had inserted a small wireless earpiece, which would allow for constant communication. Sam had a black backpack that held the necessary tools needed to enter the building.

After trying two of the overhead doors, Robert located the third door unlocked. They all entered through the door and stopped for a minute to listen for any signs of occupancy. They were all equipped with mini night-vision goggles, which permitted them to work in complete darkness. After several seconds, a faint outline of a door could

Terror from Within

be seen on the far side of the garage; light from a room behind the door, spilled into the room.

They slowly approached the door on the far side of the garage. They couldn't hear any noise coming from the other side, so Sam slowly opened the door. The door led into a hallway, and they could see several rooms on either end of the hallway. Robert went to the left in search of the office, while Sam proceeded down the hallway to the right. John followed Robert as they went from room to room looking for what they had come for. Robert clicked a button located on his belt buckle and advised the others that he had located the main office. The office had many cubicles, and each one had a desktop computer. It was going to be impossible to take all the computers, so they began looking through every drawer and file folder. After another minute or two, Sam located what they had come for. He grabbed a large binder and a laptop computer that was sitting next to it. Sam signaled to the others to make their way to the exit. John located an open cash register near the entrance that contained some US currency. He stuffed the cash into his jacket as he ran towards the loading dock. They exited the garage and shut the door. A few minutes later, they were cruising north on Interstate 94 en route to the diner.

෴

The Clearwater Police Department was notified of a burglary that had occurred sometime during the past evening. The general manager had arrived at work at 7:14 a.m. to find several drawers disturbed and several items missing. A patrol officer took the initial report and didn't summon a detective to process the scene because only a computer and a small amount of cash were taken, according to the manager. The patrol officer was an ET and he took digital photographs of the scene. The officer processed the scene for fingerprints using mostly magnetic fingerprint powder. He was unable to locate any latent fingerprints or any other usable evidence.

The general manager told the patrol officer that the night manager had neglected to lock the overhead garage door, and they were currently between security companies; therefore, they didn't have a monitored alarm system.

To the patrol officer, this wasn't an abnormal occurrence. It always seemed as though these incidents happened the one time someone forgot to lock a door or activate an alarm.

As far as any leads in the burglary, it was impossible to rule out an inside job. The only puzzling thing was why the burglars would only steal one laptop and a small amount of cash. There were plenty of flat-screen televisions, computers, and other electronics that could easily have been taken during the break-in.

Without an alarm, the burglars could have been inside the yacht club all night without being noticed.

The patrol officer left the scene and completed the report later in his shift, using his laptop computer. He submitted the report to his shift commander via a secure Internet connection and continued with his routine patrol duties.

By the time the report hit the detective sergeant's desk, it would be at least a week later. With the limited amount of evidence and the lack of leads, this case was never assigned to a detective for follow-up investigation.

Chapter 6

The plan was for them to meet at their storage unit at 8:15 a.m. and ride together to the next job site. Sam had used an address found in the client database from the yacht club burglary to gather personal information of unsuspecting high rollers from the club. He planned to use this information to pull off their next job.

Robert pulled up to the entrance of the storage facility at 7:33 a.m. He drove around to the back of the storage facility and parked adjacent to their unit. John's truck was parked several spaces over, and Robert could see the service door to their unit open.

He entered their unit and saw John sitting at the small table at the back of the room.

"Johnny, how are things going with you?"

"I can't complain. How are things going with the OP?"

"Shitty. I haven't seen the kids and I'm not even allowed a visitation with them. My wife's really playing hard ball with me. I can't believe that she's not willing to work this thing out. She's thinks I've become a piece of shit and she is pushing forward with this case."

"I feel for you; I really do. I know it's gotta be tough to be away from your kids because no matter how much of a bitch your wife is, it sure would be nice to play catch with your boy or take him out to dinner."

"There isn't really anything I can do at this point. She's using all my money to pay for an attorney, and I can't afford to hire one myself. So, I'm going to get screwed over because I don't know how to play the game and manipulate the system like her lawyer does."

"I'll check around and see if anyone knows an attorney who will work without a retainer."

"I'd appreciate it."

They sat around drinking coffee and talking about the recent news that Chrysler had just announced the layoffs of another 10,000 workers. This layoff was on top of 15,000 employees who were laid off earlier in the year. This news meant the job market would be getting worse, and the already dropping home prices would continue plummeting to new record lows. The average home price in Humble County had already dropped from $215,000 to $175,000 within the past twelve months. This downward spiral caused many baby boomers to use their 401ks and other retirement investments to help pay the bills.

Meanwhile, Sam had called to report that he had watched the homeowner leave for work at 8:00 a.m. for the second day in a row. There wasn't any other movement in the house, and a phone call to the residence all but confirmed the house was empty.

They both changed into the blue jumpsuits and got into the van before leaving the storage facility at 8:24 a.m. Sam stayed in the area of their new job site and kept surveillance on the house.

The van arrived at the residence at 8:37 a.m., pulled onto the concrete driveway, and drove towards the attached

Terror from Within

five-car garage. There were no beware of dog signs and he didn't even notice any alarm signs sitting in the yard.

Robert recalled reading a recent newspaper article with statistics showing a lot of homeowners were cancelling their alarm systems due to the economy. It showed that consumers were considering this a luxury, which further solidified their chances of getting away with their burglaries.

A large white porch surrounded the front of the massive two-story brick house. The yard was landscaped and two maple trees stood near the east property line.

Robert backed his van up to the garage door and put it in park. A small berm in the front yard, used to cover the septic system, hid the garage from the road.

John approached the front door and knocked for a few seconds. After two minutes and no answer, he retreated to the garage service door. He peered inside, and there weren't any cars in the garage. On the far wall, he could see several high-end garage storage organizers. Several pieces of lawn equipment sat against the near wall, and adjacent to that was a pegboard secured to the wall that contained an assortment of hand tools. In the corner was a flat-screen television mounted to the wall. The floor of the garage was covered in a shiny epoxy coating, the type usually installed in commercial garages.

John turned the handle to the door and found it locked. He grabbed his crowbar and a screwdriver. Several seconds later, he had the door popped open, and they both entered the garage.

They began opening cabinets and rummaged through every drawer in the garage. Robert went to the flat-screen television and unscrewed the cable. Then he grabbed his screwdriver and worked to remove the bolts that held the television to the wall mount. A minute later, the last screw was removed, and the television was free from the wall. He set the television near the service door and grabbed a circular saw, cordless drill, and a small metal toolbox filled with miscellaneous tools. He quickly brought all these items to his van and placed them inside the back door.

With most of the items from inside the garage already in his van, he proceeded to the interior door of the residence. As with most interior garage doors, only the exterior garage door was locked; the interior doors were mostly left unlocked.

Sam was still maintaining surveillance on the house and hadn't noticed anyone witnesses to the burglary.

John checked the chrome knob, and it turned freely in his hand. He gave it a slight push, and the door opened into a mudroom. He entered the mudroom with Robert right on his heels.

A split second later, an ear-piercing siren jolted them out of their complacency. With the noise came a vibrating sensation that seemed as though someone was using a gas-powered jackhammer on their ear drums. They both froze for several seconds before regaining their composure.

Just as they turned to exit the door, John spotted a silhouette of a person moving quickly down from the second floor. From the silhouette, John could see that the person was holding a long object in his or her hand.

John and Robert both darted out of the mudroom and were almost to the far side of the garage when a loud

Terror from Within

bang erupted from behind them. The casing for the service door splintered into a thousand pieces as John frantically reached for the door handle. Another loud bang erupted, and a chunk of drywall hit John in the face.

The gunshots made it apparent that this homeowner was determined to stop them. John's vision had narrowed, and his fine motor skills were beginning to diminish. He fumbled with the door handle and was finally able to open the door. As he swung the door open, he could hear the homeowner behind him, yelling something that was indiscernible.

Robert's ears were ringing so loudly that he couldn't hear himself think. His heart was thumping out of his chest, and it felt as though someone was sitting on his stomach. This made breathing somewhat of a chore and slowed his retreat to his van.

Robert hopped into the front seat of the van, and John dove into the passenger seat as Robert slammed it into gear and took off down the driveway. Robert tried to calm himself, as the last thing they needed was to crash his van and ruin their chances of a clean getaway.

He pulled onto Grand River and had traveled close to two miles before he noticed red and blue emergency lights approaching them head on. All of the vehicles on the roadway, including the white panel van, pulled over to the side of the road to allow a Humble County sheriff's deputy to pass them.

∽∾

Robert flipped open the paper, and a headline at the bottom of the front page caught his eye. The article read: "Cops seek suspect in home invasion." The opening paragraph said the sheriff's office was looking for a white van that was used in the home invasion. Robert's head began to spin, and the article slowly faded out of focus. His thoughts turned to letting his family down. This couldn't be happening, he thought, as he tried to regain his focus. Robert read the article again and it became clear to him that the past few months of running with Sam and his crew needed to end. The press release from the sheriff's office said there were numerous witnesses in the area who recalled seeing a white panel-style van in the area during the home invasion. To make matters worse, the detective sergeant who was interviewed said the sheriff's office had gathered valuable evidence at the scene and, with witness statements, they were close to arresting the offenders.

The risk was too high to keep the van around or even to drive it out of the storage facility.

Robert picked up his phone from the nightstand and hit the speed dial button to reach Sam. After two rings, Sam answered the phone.

"Sam, did you have a chance to see the results from yesterday?" Robert was cautious not to make any incriminating statements over the unsecured phone line.

"Yes. We need to meet at home this evening."

"Okay, I'll be there." Robert didn't wait for an answer as he pressed the end button.

Robert was confident that Sam would make a phone call to Gomez, and he would have one of his people get rid of the van.

Chapter 7
Monday June 19th in Three Forks, Michigan

Bailiff Andy Thompson arrived at the Humble County Government Center just after 7:30 a.m. He parked his Ford truck in a reserved parking space on the north side of the government building. He exited his truck and grabbed the ceramic coffee cup before shutting the door behind him. A quick press of his keyless remote and he heard the chirp, indicating that the truck had locked successfully.

He entered the courthouse through the public security entrance on the north side of the building.

"Good morning, Chuck," Thompson said to the court security officer who was assigned to the north entrance.

Chuck had retired from the Belcher Police Department in 2006 with thirty years of police experience. He began working full time as a court security officer because of the health benefits this new job provided.

"Morning, Andy, can't beat the weather today," Chuck replied as he glanced out the double glass doors.

Chuck and Bailiff Thompson had worked for separate police departments throughout their careers, but they were also fortunate enough to work together on several high-profile cases.

"I'm living the dream every day I come to this place," Thompson stated sarcastically as continued through the security screening area.

Thompson had also taken the full-time job with court security because his retirement health plan was costing him a fortune. He still had one son in high school and the cost of purchasing private family medical coverage was out of the question.

"Have a great day," Chuck said as he turned to greet the people who had filed in behind Thompson.

Thompson walked down the long hallway and then took the elevator downstairs to the judges' chambers. He was assigned to provide security for Judge Brown's courtroom. He always liked a change of pace, and this provided relief from the daily grind of providing security at one of the main entrances to the government center.

The elevator door opened, and Thompson strolled down the carpeted hallway before he came to the door leading into Judge Brown's chambers. He used his electronic keycard to open the door.

Thompson entered the law library. On the far wall hung picture frames of all the current judges presiding in the 53rd district court. On either side of the picture frames were massive oak bookcases that contained every Michigan compiled statutes book ever printed. There were also hundreds of books relating to current law and case law.

Terror from Within

Thompson placed his coffee cup on the rectangular conference table and took a seat in one of the executive leather chairs that sat around the table. He reached over and picked up the daily summary report, which detailed the previous day's activities. The court security officers were still sworn police officers and, therefore, were able to enforce state laws. Several people had been arrested the day before by court security for attempting to bring illegal drugs into the government center. A few items that were banned from the courthouse, including bottled water and a pocket knife, had been confiscated as well.

A few minutes later, the other bailiffs arrived and took seats around the conference table. The day's pleasantries were exchanged, and the chief of court security, Todd Betts, entered the room to begin the morning's roll call.

Chief Betts went over the previous day's activity and brought up several important upcoming court cases. He ended the short roll call and wished everyone a great day.

Thompson stood up from his chair and grabbed his coffee cup. He left the study and headed towards Judge Brown's private office.

Judge Brown had presided over felony cases in Humble County for as long as Thompson could remember. When he was working as a police officer, several of his own investigations had come before Judge Brown. Judge Brown was well respected in the community and always seemed to run a fair and balanced courtroom.

Thompson walked down the well-lit hallway and knocked on Judge Brown's door.

"Come in," said the muffled voice from behind the large mahogany door.

Thompson entered the office and saw Judge Brown sitting behind his large oak desk, staring intently at his flat-screen computer monitor.

"Good morning, Andy."

"Good morning, your honor. How was your weekend?"

"Come check out these photos."

Thompson walked around the desk and peered at the photographs on the screen. There were several pictures of king salmon, and the biggest one looked to be about twenty to twenty-five pounds.

"Wow, those fish are enormous," Thompson exclaimed as his mouth dropped open. "Were those caught on your boat?"

"Yeah, we went fishing last weekend in Columbia, and it was the best fishing I've ever had."

During the weekends in the summer, you could always find Judge Brown at his summer cottage in Columbia, which was located on Lake Michigan. The area was well known for its great fishing and summer festivals. Judge Brown would take his twenty-nine-foot *Seaswirl* out on Lake Michigan and troll for king salmon and Coho. He had even offered to take Thompson on a weekend fishing trip, but Thompson hadn't been able to fit it into his schedule.

"I'll definitely have to take you up on that fishing offer," Thompson grinned as he continued looking at the previous weekend's catch.

Terror from Within

"You're welcome anytime. We're out there all summer. You should let me know which weekend you're available because the summer will be over before you know it."

Thompson reached down and pulled his cell phone out of his pocket. He typed a reminder into his phone to check with his wife to see what weekend he could head out to Columbia for a weekend fishing trip.

Thompson glanced down at his watch as it turned 7:57 a.m. The judge saw him check his watch and quickly closed out the file of pictures. Judge Brown put on his black robe and he turned off the lights as they filed out of the office.

They made small talk as they walked down the hallway in the opposite direction of the study. They reached an elevator at the far end of the hallway, and Thompson pressed the directional arrow that pointed towards the first floor. There was a soft pinging noise, and the doors silently slid open. The judge entered the elevator first, and Thompson followed. The doors closed behind them, and Thompson pressed the button for the first floor. With a slight lurch, they were whisked to a private passageway, which was located behind the courtrooms.

When the elevator came to a stop, the doors slid silently open and they exited the elevator and walked down the hallway to the left. Thompson walked in front, and when they reached the end of the hallway, Judge Brown took a seat in a big wooden chair. Thompson entered courtroom A101 through a rear door and closed it behind him.

The courtroom was packed for the 8:00 a.m. court call. Most of these cases were going to be continued to another date, and the courtroom would empty out rather quickly, Thompson thought. He said good morning to the court reporter who was sitting behind the bench and near the judge's chair. He approached one of the assistant state's attorneys and confirmed that they were ready for the judge to begin hearing cases.

Judge Brown was summoned and he entered the courtroom.

"All rise," Thompson said to the overflow crowd. In almost perfect unison, everyone in the courtroom stood up, and Judge Brown took his seat behind the bench.

"Be seated," Judge Brown said as he looked over several pieces of paper in front of him.

The entire bench area was constructed of oak veneer and was an impressive sight for anyone who was in the courtroom for the first time. The seal of Michigan hung on the wall behind the judge, and an American flag sat off to the side.

The courtroom was wired with surveillance cameras, and several open microphones recorded all conversations near the bench. A court security officer who also provided security near the south entrance of the courthouse intermittently monitored the cameras. The audio recording allowed for the transcription of all court proceedings.

Judge Brown went alphabetically through the morning court call. As the judge called the defendants' names, they lined up at the front of the witness benches and waited to approach the judge. Several defense attorneys were milling around like vultures waiting for their clients' cases to be heard.

As each case was called, the defendant was asked if he or she was going to plead guilty or innocent to the charges that were filed against them. In all but a few of the cases, the defendants stated they wanted to plead innocent, and the judge was forced to set a future court date for a status hearing.

In the remaining cases, the defendants' attorneys hadn't arrived in the courtroom, and their cases were passed until counsel was present.

After going through the court call one time, the judge was left with about twenty people still waiting for their attorneys to arrive.

Judge Brown exited the bench and took a short recess. Thompson unlocked the large mahogany door behind him and spoke briefly with the correctional officer in the other room.

After a ten-minute break, Judge Brown re-entered the courtroom and resumed the court call by calling on the first defendant who was in custody.

The large mahogany door opened into the courtroom, and a middle-aged, white male, dressed in an orange jumpsuit, shuffled through the opening.

Chapter 8

As soon as the fleeing suspects ran out of the courtroom, Bailiff Thompson frantically barked commands over his portable radio. He didn't remember exactly what he said other than to ramble on about gunmen and an officer needing assistance in courtroom A101.

The other court security officers heard the call for assistance and most of them immediately ran towards the commotion in courtroom A101.

The first two court security personnel to arrive saw five subjects, one wearing an orange jumpsuit, running down the hall towards the rear emergency exit.

Both court security officers took off in pursuit of the subjects. They were able to use their portable radios to update the responding court security officers on the location of the fleeing suspects.

One of the court security officers, who had recently retired from his job as a Michigan state trooper and was still in decent shape, had gained some ground on the subjects.

As the suspects neared the emergency exit, one of them quickly turned around and fired several bursts from his assault rifle. The lead officer stopped running and took cover behind a brick column located in the hallway. Several of the rounds struck the column right in front of the officer. Several more rounds lodged themselves into the drywall several feet away, showering the hallway with white drywall dust.

The officer peered around the column and was able to fire several rounds down the hallway towards the exit. The subjects were probably seventy-five yards away, and with his 9mm handgun, he knew his chance of hitting a moving target from that distance was next to impossible.

Just outside of the exit to the government center, a dark-green panel van pulled up to the curb; the side door slid open. All five subjects piled into the van, and it sped off just as the door slammed shut.

The court security officer relayed a description of the fleeing van over his portable radio. Another court security officer who was in charge of relaying the information to the Humble County dispatchers was preoccupied with securing the building and he wasn't able to relay the message to the sheriff's dispatch center.

The delay in the dispatchers receiving the information allowed precious time to pass without any local police agencies on the lookout for the fleeing green van.

☙❧

The green van turned out of the government center and drove west down Grand River Avenue towards M-59. Within minutes, it turned south onto M-59 and headed towards Interstate 96. The driver continued driving the speed limit as the police scanner mounted inside the van hadn't yet broadcast a description of their getaway vehicle. The occupants of the van even slowed down several times to allow a squad car, with its emergency lights and sirens activated, to pass them going in the opposite direction.

Terror from Within

The driver turned on the van's blinker and merged onto the interstate.

☙❧

The area in and around the courthouse was soon swarming with police officers from all over the area.

Chief Betts had heard the frantic calls over his Motorola radio and had sprinted all the way from the far side of the government center. He had ordered his guys to secure all entrances and exits to the courthouse. The order was for nobody to enter or exit the government building under any circumstance. He needed time to stabilize the situation and make sure there weren't any additional attacks planned.

Meanwhile, Chief of Corrections Chief Kowalski ordered a lockdown of the entire correctional facility to prevent any further acts of violence. The prisoners, who were down near the courtrooms waiting for their cases to be heard, were immediately whisked back to their assigned jail cells.

Chief Betts was on his second career in law enforcement. He had entered the Washtenaw Community College Police Academy at the age of twenty-one. He was hired by the Clinton Police Department after completing the sixteen-week police-training program. He had held almost every position at the department, including field-training officer, detective, sergeant, and eventually shift commander.

In his twenty-five years of experience in law enforcement, he hadn't responded to anything of this magnitude. There were always robberies and domestics, but no active shooter cases or anything similar to this incident.

Chief Betts arrived at courtroom A101 four minutes after the subjects had fled the area. He saw paramedics attending to the fallen police officer. It was obvious the officer had sustained fatal injuries. To preserve the officer's dignity, a white sheet was finally placed over his body.

Several court security officers ushered the witnesses, who had the unfortunate luck of being in the courtroom during the shooting and subsequent escape, to a separate waiting area near the grand jury room. The responding detectives would interview the witnesses separately, and it was essential they be detained for a short time.

Once the courtroom was cleared of all witnesses, yellow crime-scene tape was secured around each door.

Responding rescue personnel were summoned to the waiting area because two elderly females were experiencing heart attack symptoms.

Three court security officers were assigned to provide scene security for the courtroom. Their main concern was to make sure nobody entered the courtroom and compromised the crime scene.

The entire hallway outside of courtroom A101 was cordoned off by more yellow crime-scene tape.

Chief Betts initially took command of the incident and designated the government center atrium as a staging area for responding agencies.

EMTs from the Three Forks Fire Department were on standby for any medical issues that might arise during the course of the investigation.

Chief Betts's Motorola earpiece crackled, and a familiar voice came over the radio.

Terror from Within

"Chief, it's the sheriff; I'll be down in the atrium in a few minutes. Please let everyone know we'll be holding a briefing shortly."

Sheriff Ward Calhoun had been elected sheriff of Humble County in 1990. He was the county's longest-running sheriff and was well known throughout the community. He ran a very professional and well-respected law enforcement agency. The department's morale was running at an all-time high, and it appeared as though he would hold the top position at the sheriff's department until he decided to retire.

"Sheriff, a command post has been set up, and all responding agencies are currently reporting to me," Chief Betts replied, glancing out the large double-paned windows.

It was sunny, and temperatures were expected to reach into the high eighties. The chief had scheduled his normal Tuesday golf game for later in the afternoon, and he tried to keep his mind from wandering away from the events that were unfolding in front of him.

Finally, an all-points bulletin was broadcast over the sheriff's office's 800-megahertz radio system to be on the lookout for the dark-green, panel-style van. A sheriff's deputy who had initially responded to the courthouse for the shooting relayed over his radio that he had noticed a similar-style van heading south on M-59 towards Interstate 96.

Two Michigan State Police troopers were dispatched to the interstate to try to locate the fleeing van.

Chapter 9

Sheriff Calhoun disseminated a message to the commanders of all divisions, within the sheriff's office that a briefing on this incident would begin at 10:00 a.m. in the government center atrium.

By this time, the sheriff's dispatchers had been overwhelmed with telephone inquiries from local, regional, and national news agencies. With the way news traveled over the Internet, it wasn't long before the news agencies arrived at the government center to get live shots of the action as it unfolded.

The sheriff's office had their public relations deputies set up a media-staging outlet at the Buckley Middle School across the street from the government center.

The media vans arrived just as fast as the responding detectives. They parked their vehicles in the large parking lot at the school and raised their massive antennas. The reporters rushed to the grassy area near Grand River Avenue to get the best view of the government center and the investigators milling about.

At the same time, Channel 2 and Channel 7's news helicopters began hovering above, providing their respective networks with live feeds.

The sheriff held his briefing in the atrium at 10:00 a.m. with all of the responding agencies. He started out by having a moment of silence for the fallen police officer, an eight-year veteran of the Three Forks Police Department.

After the moment of silence, the sheriff went into the details of the morning's events. The now-escaped suspect had been arrested the month before by the Humble County Sheriff's Office on an outstanding warrant for home invasion. The suspect was wanted for breaking into an elderly couple's home and tying them up at gunpoint. The suspect took all of the couple's jewelry and cash before fleeing their residence.

The prisoner had a court date scheduled for earlier this morning, at 8:30 a.m. He had entered the courtroom dressed in his standard-issue orange jumpsuit. He was secured with shackles on his hands and legs. The sheriff explained how an unarmed correctional officer led the suspect into the courtroom to the bench in front of Judge Brown.

For an unknown reason, the prisoner fell to the ground and curled up into a fetal position. At that time, four armed individuals took control of the courtroom and shot a police officer before leaving the area with the prisoner.

The sheriff continued by telling everyone that the suspects had fled the courthouse with several court security officers in pursuit, at which time one of the offenders turned around and fired several more rounds from an assault rifle.

The sheriff reminded everyone in attendance to pray for the fallen officer, and that they would leave no stone unturned in an attempt to locate and apprehend the offenders of this heinous act.

Terror from Within

The green van pulled into a rest stop located on Interstate 96, east of Three Forks. The rest stop was set back in a wooded section off the interstate.

The van continued to the right and drove down the truck lane, which went behind the rest stop building. Fortunately, for the occupants in the van, there were no semi trucks parked in the rear lot.

The van slowed down and pulled into a parking space along the back of the lot.

The passengers had already changed into new clothes and had placed their old clothes into two black, industrial-strength garbage bags. They piled the black garbage bags into the corner and exited the van. One of the subjects grabbed a spray bottle from behind the driver's seat and sprayed the inside with gasoline.

The first suspect rolled down the driver's window of the van and shut the door. He pulled out a match and lit it before tossing it through the open window of the van.

❧❧

Blake had taken the day off and was at home packing the family's SUV for a planned trip to the Upper Peninsula. Maria was quickly cleaning the house so it wouldn't be a total disaster when they returned from the trip.

They loved to explore the vast areas of the northern Lower Peninsula and Upper Peninsula. They had previously attended the cherry festival in Traverse City and the tulip festival in Holland.

They were scheduled to camp at a state park situated on the shores of Lake Michigan, overlooking the Mackinaw Bridge. The Mackinaw Bridge, the largest suspension bridge in the Western hemisphere, was built in 1957 and spanned five miles over Lake Michigan. This bridge is the only connection between Michigan's two peninsulas.

Blake's thoughts drifted to the ferry ride they would be taking across Lake Huron to Mackinaw Island, situated just east of Michigan's Upper Peninsula. Automobiles are not allowed on Mackinaw Island, and they were looking forward to a nice, peaceful horse-drawn carriage ride around the island.

They both needed this vacation to recharge their batteries. With Michigan's economy in the worst shape in history, it was taking its toll on their family. With the constant threat of layoffs and funding cuts, Blake never knew when he would walk into work and be handed a pink slip.

Blake was loading the SUV as if he was building a puzzle, meticulously fitting everything inside, when his cell phone rang. He placed the suitcase he was carrying on the floor of the garage and unclipped the cell phone from his belt. He glanced at the caller ID and initially thought about not answering the call.

"Hello?"

"Hi, Blake; it's McGuire. Do you have a minute?" Sergeant McGuire asked as if Blake really had a choice.

"Sure, go ahead."

"We've just had an attack on the government center. Four armed gunmen took over one of the courtrooms and managed to kill a police officer. Then they were able to flee with a prisoner who was in the courtroom." He paused for a second to let his comments sink in. "I know you took the next week off, and I'm not going to force you to cancel your vacation, but..." was all Sergeant McGuire could get out before Blake interrupted him.

"Holy shit! Our trip can wait; I'll let Maria know and I'll be en route shortly."

"I'm sorry to bother you with this incident; it's just that we do really need as much assistance as possible. I really appreciate it," Sergeant McGuire exclaimed.

McGuire quickly filled him in on the current status of the investigation. Detectives from the Michigan State Police, Humble County Sheriff's Office, and several other local agencies were beginning the tedious process of interviewing each and every witness. He thanked Blake again for dropping everything to assist with the investigation and hung up the phone.

Shit, Blake thought as he closed the cell phone and clipped it back on his belt. He looked at the suitcase for several seconds as he pondered how to break the news to Maria. He knew it wasn't going to go over very well, and he placed the suitcase in the back of the SUV.

He shut the rear hatch and slowly walked towards the door to the house. He was sure she'd understand the circumstances surrounding this incident. It wasn't every day that a police officer was murdered in cold blood in Humble County. These suspects needed to be apprehended as quickly as possible. The danger they posed was far too great to allow the investigation to drag on for several weeks.

He climbed the two steps and turned the chrome door handle. The door slid open and Blake could hear Maria telling the children to use the bathroom prior to the trip. "Why does this kind of thing occur right before my vacation?" he thought as he closed the door behind him. He slipped off his shoes and walked towards the bathroom.

He paused for a second and gathered his thoughts. "There is a slight change of plans."

"What do you mean, 'a slight change of plans'?" she responded with a stern look on her face.

"I just received a phone call from Sergeant McGuire. Some armed men just killed a police officer at the government center and they fled the area with a prisoner."

"Wow—how did that happen?"

"I'm not exactly sure at this point. McGuire just gave me the basics and asked if I could assist them. I can't leave the department shorthanded and just take off knowing that a major investigation was going on at the office. Hopefully, these guys will be caught soon, and then we could still go on the trip." Blake knew the probability of this actually occurring was slim, but he needed to sugarcoat this to make sure Maria wasn't going to be pissed about using up her vacation to watch the children for a few days.

"How do you know they'll be caught soon?" Maria asked with a look of doubt on her face.

"I can't say for sure, but these guys need to be caught, and I would hate for them to cause harm to one of my family members."

"What about the reservations?"

"Can you call them to explain that it's an emergency? Tell them that we'll definitely reschedule later this summer."

"I'll give it a try," Maria added as she shrugged her shoulders. "I'm glad I used my vacations days to stay home and watch the kids," Maria mumbled under her breath.

Blake reached over and slid his arms around her waist. She had always stayed in shape, even after the children were born. She prided herself on staying in shape while maintaining a full-time job and being a parent. He moved his head close to hers and kissed her gently.

"I love you, dear, and I'm sorry to disappoint you," Blake said as he pulled her tight against his body. "I'll make this up to you once this case is wrapped up." He winked at her and gave her another kiss.

She kissed him again and said, "Well, you better get going because the faster you get to the office, the faster you can make this up to me." She had a smirk on her face as he let go of her and hustled to change into a new set of clothes.

Blake threw on a pair of blue jeans and polo shirt with the sheriff's department logo on the right breast. He pulled his compact .40 caliber Sig Sauer out of the gun safe and inserted a loaded magazine. He slid the magazine into the well until it clicked into place. He released the slide on the gun and a bullet was inserted into the chamber. He slid the gun into a black paddle holster and secured it to his waist with a belt. He secured his badge to the belt along with an extra magazine and a pair of handcuffs. He went into the kitchen and grabbed his car keys.

Blake found the children playing with toys in the living room. He quickly gave the children hugs and kisses. "Good-bye; Daddy loves you guys. Be good for Mommy, okay?" They gave him hugs, and he left the living room.

"Good-bye, dear," Blake said as he reached the service door to the garage. "I love you."

"I love you, too," Maria yelled from the other room.

"I'll give you a call once I have a better timeframe on the progress of the case."

"Be safe out there for me."

Blake entered the garage and jumped into his car. He hit the button on the garage door opener, and the door slowly opened up. He pulled out of the driveway and was soon cruising towards the government center.

Blake arrived at the government center just as the clock in his car turned 9:43 a.m. He met with Sergeant McGuire, who briefed him on what occurred earlier in the morning. He was assigned the task of reviewing the prisoner's background, including the reason for his current incarceration and any known associates, and to search the jail cell of the now-escaped prisoner.

He checked the prisoner's prior criminal history, which only had one theft charge and two charges for disorderly conduct. He was being held on a home invasion charge when he escaped.

Blake ran a search for the prisoner's name and came back with the report numbers for each of the previous contacts law enforcement had with this subject. Getting copies of the reports would take some time, as he would have to make telephone calls to the individual departments who had taken the initial reports. A representative from those departments would have to go to their records division to pull the reports and make copies before faxing them over to Blake.

While checking prior law enforcement contacts with this subject, he was able to locate several other people who could possibly be associated with the escapee. Blake wrote those names and addresses down as possible leads.

Blake then called over to the correctional facility and advised them that he was going to be stopping over

Terror from Within

to search the jail cell of the escaped prisoner. He grabbed a quick drink from the water cooler and tossed his paper cup into the wastebasket.

He briskly walked across the government center and entered the main lobby of the jail. There was a black button on the wall near a bulletproof glass window, and Blake pressed it to summon someone in central control.

A short time later, a voice came over the intercom and advised Blake that a sergeant would be down to escort him to the appropriate jail cell.

Blake sat down on a gray plastic chair in the lobby and waited for the arrival of the correctional sergeant. At the far end of the lobby, there was another set of large windows that overlooked the jail's visiting area.

The correctional facility held regular visiting hours for its inmates, and the visits were conducted through a video conference. This system allowed the inmate to be in another place in the jail and still be able to speak with any visitors. This also decreased the number of times inmates were moved throughout the jail, increasing the overall efficiency.

While looking at the video conferencing system, Blake made a mental note to review all of the escaped prisoner's visitors.

Blake heard a faint buzzing noise, and the door near the intercom system opened; a female sergeant stepped through the doorway. Blake remembered running into this sergeant on several other occasions when he needed to have criminal complaints notarized. She was always friendly and willing to assist with anything she could.

"Right this way," she said, pointing through the doorway and gesturing for Blake to come in.

"Thank you for coming down here so quick. We've all had such a hectic day and I'm sure you have many other things to do," he replied, getting up from the plastic chair. He walked through the large steel door.

"Nothing is more important than this investigation; anything else at this point becomes secondary," she replied.

They walked down the block corridor, and he heard a loud thud as the steel door slammed shut behind them.

The entire correctional facility was monitored by a closed-circuit surveillance system and included voice monitoring in most of the locations. This allowed for the correctional officers in the central control office to monitor all the cameras as well as any conversations between inmates and correctional officers.

The large steel security doors were all accessed by an intercom system, and at each set of doors, central control had to approve access before the door would unlock.

They continued walking down what seemed to Blake like endless hallways of bricks and mortar. He had only traveled deep inside the correctional facility on a few occasions, and it always seemed be more confusing each time he was past the booking area.

It didn't take long for Blake to realize why nobody had ever successfully escaped from this facility. With the number of cameras and security features, the general public could sure rest safe at night knowing that the chances of someone escaping were slim to none.

Terror from Within

Blake continued following the sergeant until the hallway ended, and they began climbing a set of stairs. They reached the second floor and were buzzed through another set of steel doors.

They arrived at cellblock seven, which had a maximum population of fifty inmates. Two correctional officers who were stationed within the cellblock monitored the inmates. The officers were assigned the duty of keeping the peace amongst the always-changing population.

During this particular visit, the entire block was on lockdown, and the only jail cell that was unoccupied was now a crime scene.

Blake walked up a set of steel grated stairs and walked past the rows of cells. A few of the inmates had seen him enter, and they were eager to throw an insult at the detective. As he passed the cells, the inmates plastered themselves against their bars and taunted Blake.

"Come in here, you piece of shit" one of them yelled as he tried to urinate through the bars. "Take that badge off and I bet you ain't such a bad ass."

Blake knew better than to try to respond to their crude comments. He just stared straight ahead and continued towards the far end of the block. It wasn't worth the headache of egging them on because there wasn't anything to gain from that sort of encounter.

There was more profanity and derogatory comments aimed towards Blake, and a few of the inmates even tried to grab him as he walked by.

He walked near the handrails of the balcony until he reached the jail cell he had arrived to search.

Blake reached over and pulled his digital camera out of his back pocket. He stood back and took photographs of the outside of the jail cell.

From where he stood, he could see one steel bunk bed on each side of the room. In the center, there was a steel toilet that didn't have a seat. Connected to the toilet was a steel sink that contained two basic handles for water. Above the toilet was a small window about six inches tall and one foot wide.

Each of the beds had a thin blue mattress pad and an orange wool blanket. Blake could see two toothbrushes and a tube of toothpaste on the sink.

The walls were painted white and were of cinderblock construction. The ceiling had one set of recessed lights, which were covered by a steel cage to prevent anyone from tampering with them. The gray tile floor had a drain in the middle to allow for easy cleanup.

Blake entered the room and took more photographs of the inside of the cell. He photographed everything, including the drain on the floor.

He turned the digital camera off and returned it to his rear pocket. He pulled a pair of blue latex gloves from his other pocket and placed them on his hands. He then began the meticulous process of searching every square inch of the jail cell. He checked under the toilet and sink and wasn't able to find anything suspicious. Nothing appeared to be wrong with the power outlet or the recessed lights.

He overturned the mattresses and thoroughly examined each one to make sure there wasn't anything hidden inside. After separating the bedding and placing everything on the floor, Blake searched every crack and corner of the steel bed frame.

While searching the second bunk bed, he located an irregularity in the frame that he didn't see in the first bed. Upon closer examination, he discovered part of the steel had been ground away and was now covered by a paper-like substance. The substance's color didn't exactly match the rest of the bed frame, and that's what drew Blake's attention to that spot.

He pulled out his camera and took close up photographs of the irregularity in the bed frame. He pulled out his pocketknife and chipped away at the material. The material flaked and fell to the floor. He kept scrapping away at the material, and soon a hole, the size of a deck of cards, was uncovered. Blake reached his hand slowly into the hole and felt the weight of something hanging from a string just inside. He pulled on the string and, to his amazement, a cell phone came into view.

Chapter 10

As the two Michigan state troopers were searching up and down the interstate for the green van, a passing motorist called 911 to report a fire coming from the area of the rest stop east of Three Forks. One of the troopers turned his squad car around in the center median and started towards the reported fire.

The traffic at the rest areas was usually light during the middle of the workweek, and he didn't anticipate any other cars in the parking lot.

As the trooper approached, he could see a dark plume of smoke rising above the trees near the rest stop. He called over his radio and informed his dispatchers that he was pulling up on scene just as he merged onto the exit ramp for the rest stop.

As the trooper rounded the corner, he could see a fully engulfed vehicle fire on the far side of parking lot. He updated his dispatchers and took a quick glance around the area for any other signs of activity. There was a small car parked in the front parking lot.

As he looked back at the burning vehicle, his heart skipped a beat because it matched the description of the getaway van used in the government center escape. He notified dispatch that the burning van was most likely the one used in the attack. His partner responded over the radio that he was now en route to the rest stop.

Detective Lieutenant Young of the Humble County Sheriff's Office was canvassing the interstate while monitoring the troopers' radio frequency and he immediately drove toward the rest area. He pulled out his cell phone and called the command post at the government center to put out the word that he would need an evidence technician and a photographer sent over to the rest stop on Interstate 96.

The trooper parked his squad car a short distance from the burning vehicle and opened the trunk of his car. He grabbed a fire extinguisher from the trunk and approached the vehicle. He hadn't seen anyone else in the area and he wanted to make sure someone wasn't trapped inside of the vehicle.

The trooper could hear the sirens of the responding fire trucks approaching as he neared the van. The smoke and intense fire kept him from getting any closer than fifteen feet. He pulled the pin on the fire extinguisher and aimed the nozzle at the driver's side window. He squeezed the trigger and swept the area around the window.

As he felt the pressure of the fire extinguisher slowing to a trickle, the first responding fire engine pulled around the bend on the ramp to the rest stop.

The engine parked near the burning van, and the firefighters grabbed the red hose off the side of the fire truck. The driver ran the pump and sent water rushing down to the end of the three-quarter-inch hose. Two fire fighters, who were dressed in full turn out gear, including the Self Contained Breathing Apparatus (SCBA), ad-

Terror from Within

vanced the hose line towards the raging inferno. The lead fire fighter pulled back on the nozzle, and a blast of water sprung from the end of the hose.

They were able to extinguish the fire within a few minutes, and all that was left was a burned-out shell of the van.

The second responding trooper shut down the entrance to the rest stop to help preserve the area as a possible crime scene. It was still unknown if anyone was inside of the rest stop's building, which housed restrooms and various vending machines.

The first trooper kept an eye on the building as he waited for backup to arrive.

Two Humble County sheriff's deputies had been dispatched to the area and arrived on scene just after the fire was extinguished.

The rest stop building was a one-story brown brick building. On the north and south sides, there was a set of double glass doors. On each side of the doors, there were large windows. The rest of the building consisted of small smoked-out windows, which were up high, signifying the bathroom portion of the building.

One of the deputies had his dispatchers check the Michigan Department of Transportation's contact list to see if there was a telephone inside of the building. The dispatchers weren't able to locate a telephone number for the building. The chances of there being a telephone inside were slim, but they had to see if they could make contact with someone inside.

The suspects had all fled the government center in the green panel van and, at this point, there was no way to tell if the police had come across the van while the subjects were inside using the bathroom.

Detective Lieutenant Young arrived on scene and relieved the second trooper, who was securing the entrance to the rest area. Detective Lieutenant Young called the sheriff's dispatchers and advised them to start the activation process for the SWAT team. He knew there wasn't any need to rush this situation if the suspects were, in fact, still inside the building.

The second trooper pulled his squad car further into the parking lot and met with the other officers as they formulated a plan to secure a perimeter around the building where the Humble County SWAT team could assemble.

All four officers tactically took cover around each side of the building, using several large oak trees as cover. If someone was inside of the building with a high-powered rifle, like the ones used at the government center, they knew it wouldn't be hard for the suspects to shoot them from a long distance.

Meanwhile, the fire department backed their truck down the entrance to the rest stop and assisted with blocking the ramp. They decided to stand by and provide any assistance they could in this situation.

Lieutenant Young's message was sent, and the SWAT team members received text messages on their cell phones alerting them to the incident at the interstate rest stop. Most of the members were already called in during the initial government center escape and now responded to the sheriff's office for another briefing.

The SWAT team commander formulated a plan and briefed all of the team's members on the situation at

Terror from Within

the rest stop. Aerial photographs of the scene were disseminated, and the commander described the manner in which they would be approaching the building. He went over what each team member's responsibility would be once they arrived on scene. The first mission was to have everyone come home safely after the incident. The second objective was to quickly and effectively search the building while minimizing the risk to the officers involved. The third objective was to apprehend any possible suspects located inside of the building.

One of the SWAT team members contacted MDOT and obtained a layout of the building. He drew a rough sketch of the building and passed it out to other team members. Each entrance and exit point was going to have to be accounted for. In the case of an emergency, all members would be notified via their headsets and instructed as to the nature of the emergency.

The SWAT team would be heavily armed, and they would take every precaution necessary to take control of the situation with the least amount of force necessary.

Each member donned his or her department-issued camouflage gear, which included helmets, bullet-resistant vests, handguns, rifles, flash bangs, and smoke grenades. They filed into a non-descript black box truck in descending order. Once they arrived at the rest stop, they would need to be ready for deployment at a moment's notice.

The sheriff's office utilizes an Armored Personnel Carrier for use in hostage or high-risk situations. The kind of brazen criminals who had taken over the courtroom were the exact reason the sheriff's office had purchased the APC.

Four of the team members entered the APC and secured the hatch. They would be the first SWAT vehicle to enter the area and had been instructed by the commander to park directly in front of the building.

The APC could withstand handgun and rifle fire, as it was used by the U.S. Army to transport infantry into the battlefield during times of war. The officers inside the APC would be able to see inside the front windows of the building without sacrificing officer safety.

The caravan of SWAT vehicles started out of the government center parking lot and headed west on Grand River Avenue. As they passed the large crowd of news media, the deputies could see the looks of confusion as the cameramen frantically looked for an update on why the SWAT team was being activated.

The caravan continued south on M-59 and soon merged onto Interstate 96. It was quite the sight to see as the APC drove down the road with the black box truck and several marked squad cars in front of and behind them.

They soon reached the entrance to the rest stop and could see the fire engine blocking the entrance. The engine backed up on an angle and let the caravan of SWAT vehicles enter.

The APC continued driving around the bend in the entrance ramp, and the rest of the vehicles stopped and waited for the APC to get into position. It continued to the left and drove to the front of the building. It drove over a set of parking blocks and pulled within ten feet of the front door.

The commander looked through the video monitoring system and could see into the lobby of the building.

Terror from Within

There were numerous vending machines and a drinking fountain. There were three doors on either side of the vestibule. The doors all had hinges on the outside, meaning the doors swung outward, toward the vestibule. Therefore, they weren't going to be able to utilize their robot to search the interior of the building.

The commander tried several times to reach someone inside using a bull horn system that was mounted on the APC. After a short time, with no response, the commander radioed to the rest of the team that there wasn't any movement or response from inside of the building.

The black box truck pulled into the parking lot and stayed on the east side of the building, the side without windows, as it offered good cover for the approaching SWAT team.

The team exited the back of the box truck and briskly walked in a single-file line towards the southeast side of the building. The point man in the stack made contact with the commander inside the APC via his portable radio and verified that there still wasn't any movement from inside the building.

Once the stack was set to proceed, they all shuffled forward and neared the front entrance of the building. The time to abort the operation ended as the lead officer passed in front of the large glass window. The officer checked the glass door and found it to be unlocked. He held the door open, and the remaining SWAT team filed in through the doorway.

Chapter 11

Detective Frank Garcia was following up on leads as to how the firearms were brought into the government center. He had over twenty years with the Humble County Sheriff's Office. He began his career with the Belcher Police Department. He worked in Belcher for several years before applying to work for the sheriff's department. He wanted to work for a larger department that offered more opportunities for advancement. The Belcher PD only had one detective and one school resource officer. Garcia knew that unless an officer retired, there wasn't any room to advance his career. Garcia didn't want to be stuck on road patrol for his entire career.

So, he applied to the sheriff's office and went through their rigorous testing process. He was put through several intensive interviews with top-level supervisors. Even though he was already a police officer, a thorough background check was done, including interviews with all his neighbors about his character and any issue they might have with him.

He was subjected to psychological and polygraph examinations. His personal file at the PD was examined with a fine-tooth comb. The sheriff's office was always leery about police officers jumping ship to another department just because they thought the grass might be greener on the other side.

Garcia was eventually hired as a road patrol deputy. Five years later, he had the opportunity to transfer to the detective bureau.

Garcia met with Chief Betts in the atrium, and they retreated to the confines of the government center surveillance office. The office looked like a mini command center, as two rows of flat-screen monitors showed almost every angle from in and around the government center. Several of the monitors had little speakers mounted near them, which indicated the presence of voice recordings in that particular area of the government center. The entrances of the government center and all of the courtrooms were wired for audio recordings.

The room was about ten feet wide and fifteen feet long. On one end was a large dry-erase board, which had several dates and times written in the corner. Next to the dates and times were names of defendants in upcoming court cases.

Usually, when a high-profile court case was in session, it was common practice for a court security officer to monitor the court proceedings to make sure there weren't any public safety concerns.

"On a normal work day, we usually have two court security officers who are constantly monitoring all of these cameras," Chief Betts said as he motioned towards the two swivel chairs sitting near the closest row of monitors. "There are rare instances where this room isn't being monitored at all. The issue today was we had one officer call in sick, and the second officer had stepped out to use the bathroom. It's more of a luxury to be able to have someone monitoring this surveillance system at all times. With the recent budgetary issues, we have had to pull officers from surveillance duty to cover security in a courtroom or at one of the entrances."

Garcia looked around the room. The floor was carpeted and several noise-dampening posters were hanging on the wall opposite the surveillance monitors.

"Can you pull up the surveillance video from inside courtroom A101, starting at the time the doors opened at 8:00 a.m.?" Garcia asked as he took a seat in one of the swivel chairs. "I need to get a good description of these guys. Then we can go back and see what happens when they actually enter the government center."

"With our updated metal-detection equipment, there would be no way these sorts of guns should slip through the scrutiny of the officers at one of the entrances. You know most of my guys are well-trained retired police officers. The main reason we hire guys with prior experience is because they know what to look for when it comes to people acting suspiciously. Body posture, hands, and eyes tell a lot when it comes to determining if someone is up to no good."

The chief sat down in the second swivel chair and rolled up next to the keyboard, which was situated in front of a monitor. He typed in the appropriate information he needed to start the audio and video for courtroom A101, starting when the courtroom opened in the morning.

The monitor was split into four separate camera angles. The upper left view was from a camera in the hallway outside the entrance to courtroom A101. The upper right camera showed a view from the opposite end of the hallway and pointed towards the courtroom as well. The bottom left camera angle showed the entire A101 courtroom from the back of the courtroom. The bottom right camera angle, positioned behind the judge, showed the front portion of the courtroom.

"Now there are several different microphones located near the bench that are constantly recording any conversations that take place at the witness table, defense table, and on the bench directly in front of the judge. We can isolate any one of the microphones to listen in on exactly what was being said. In live mode, we have the ability to zoom in on any of the cameras to get a better view of something we see. The only downfall with this system is once the video is recorded, there is no way of zooming in on any portion of the video. One of my guys has to be physically watching the surveillance system and zooming in for this feature to do us any good."

Garcia nodded as he continued watching the screens in front of him. The courtroom was standing-room only and everyone was waiting for the arrival of Bailiff Thompson and Judge Brown.

Bailiff Thompson could be seen entering the room and scanning the crowd. He seemed to get the attention of the Assistant SA, who was tasked with prosecuting the cases in this particular courtroom. Garcia knew from previous experience that Bailiff Thompson would have been looking to make sure the SA was ready to proceed with the morning court call.

Terror from Within

Judge Brown entered the room several minutes later, and Garcia could see the entire courtroom stand up in unison.

Garcia kept scanning the crowd to see if anyone stood out, and his eyes fell on several individuals who were wearing baseball hats. This seemed odd, as most judges ordered anyone wearing hats to remove them when they were in the courtroom.

Garcia kept his eyes on these two subjects as each defendant was called to have his or her case heard in front of Judge Brown.

A short time later, Judge Brown called a recess and left the courtroom. This break allowed the SA to speak with several of the defense attorneys on issues pertaining to their clients' cases. By this time, most of the courtroom had cleared out, but there were still about twenty or so people waiting for their cases to be heard.

During this entire time, Garcia didn't see movement from the two subjects who were wearing baseball hats. They seemed to be slowly scanning the courtroom as they sat quietly in their respective benches.

"See those two guys wearing baseball hats?"

"I was just going to say that seems strange. Most judges won't allow people to wear hats in their courtrooms," Chief Betts chimed in.

"Neither of them has moved since they entered the courtroom. I was scanning over the mornings court call as Judge Brown went through it, and these guys didn't appear to acknowledge that they were here for their own court case."

Garcia continued watching the screen as Judge Brown reappeared in the courtroom, and the remaining people in the courtroom again arose simultaneously. The judge took a seat in his large oak chair and the rest of the courtroom again took their seats.

The judge resumed the court call by calling on the first inmate who was being held in a temporary jail cell directly behind the large mahogany door situated behind Bailiff Thompson.

Garcia could see the door open, and the now escaped inmate, who was dressed in the bright orange jumpsuit, entered the courtroom. Garcia witnessed for the first time what unfolded next. The inmate was called to the bench directly in front of Judge Brown. Just as the public defender argued something about his client's criminal case, the inmate doubled over and could be heard writhing in pain.

Garcia looked at the other surveillance camera's view. He saw the two subjects who were wearing the baseball hats stand up.

Two other individuals, who had been sitting casually near the front of the courtroom, also stood up and joined the first two subjects in the aisles.

"Can you pause it right there?" Garcia exclaimed.

"Sure." The chief clicked the left button on the computer mouse, and all the images paused.

Garcia unzipped his black leather binder and pulled a silver pen out of its elastic holder. On top of the legal pad he wrote the date and time from the video. He looked at the screen and analyzed each suspect's clothing and appearance.

The first subject, who was wearing a baseball hat, also had a long, black coat, blue jeans, and light-colored gym shoes. He appeared to be around six feet tall with a stocky build. His hair was short and barely stuck out below the back of the baseball hat. This subject had pulled out an assault rifle and was in the process of walking to the rear of the courtroom.

The second subject was also wearing a baseball hat and he, too, had an assault rifle which he pointed directly at Bailiff Thompson. He was dressed in khaki-colored cargo pants, dark-colored shoes, and his long, dark-colored suit coat had undoubtedly allowed him to conceal the assault rifle.

The third and fourth subjects were side by side and en route to assist the fallen inmate. They were wearing bulky tan-colored jackets, blue jeans, and dark-colored gym shoes. Neither of these subjects was wearing a hat, and the surveillance camera situated behind Judge Brown offered a somewhat clear view of their faces. Garcia didn't immediately recognize either of these two subjects.

He finished writing down the descriptions of the suspects and laid his pen on top of the legal pad. He reached into his shirt pocket and pulled out his reading glasses. He rubbed his eyes and then put the glasses on. Garcia studied the faces of both individuals to see if they would ring a bell from any previous intelligence bulletins.

After a few minutes, he realized he needed to continue watching the video. Garcia picked up his digital camera off the desk and double-checked the camera to make sure the flash was off. He took several photographs of the monitor so he could disseminate the images to the local police agencies.

Garcia quickly downloaded the photographs onto his laptop computer and saved them in a desktop folder. He attached the photographs of the suspects to the e-mail and completed a correspondence indicating the nature of the incident. He added the Regional Counter Terrorism Center as the recipient and hit the send button. The RCTC would be able to enhance the photographs and run them through their facial-recognition software. The images would then be compared to every state-issued identification and arrest record in the entire United States. They might know within twenty-four hours if any of the photographs came back with a positive match.

Garcia closed his e-mail account and turned to Chief Betts. "Okay, let's see the rest of this video."

Garcia was still trying to recall the faces of the two individuals as the chief clicked on the icon to start playing the recording. Garcia was usually pretty good at recognizing faces, and he was starting to settle on the fact that he had never personally dealt with either of these suspects in the past.

Since the first two suspects were wearing baseballs hats, he wasn't able to get a good view of their faces.

The surveillance video continued playing and they watched the entire attack unfold. Garcia made a mental note to speak with Bailiff Thompson and let him know there wasn't anything he could have done differently to stop the attack. He didn't stand a chance against several heavily armed men. Had Bailiff Thompson tried to heroically stop the attack, there would have been a lot more bloodshed in the courtroom.

They watched the rest of the scene unfold on the monitor in front of them, including the subsequent shootout in the hallway. Once this portion of the incident was over, Garcia finished taking notes on the exact times and details of the events.

"Could you please rewind the video until we see these subjects enter the courthouse?" Blake asked Chief Betts.

"I'll change the views of the surveillance cameras to include the main entrances of the courthouse. Then we can track where these guys went after entering the building," the chief said as he navigated through the surveillance program.

The camera angle showing the two main entrances of the government center popped up on the main monitor. The time stamp on the bottom of the screen showed it was 7:55 a.m.

The public entrances to the government center were opened at 8:00 a.m. every morning.

With the surveillance screen split into two sections, the video began to play. These particular surveillance cameras were mounted inside the main entrance doors and showed everyone who entered and exited the government center.

At 8:06 a.m., the first suspect appeared at the north entrance to the government center. He was wearing a long, dark overcoat and a baseball hat as he entered the front doors. In fact, the suspect blended in quite well with everyone who was entering the building, Garcia thought. From the angle of the surveillance camera, all Garcia could see was the top of the suspect's head. He wasn't able to see any of the suspect's facial features. The suspect entered the security screening desk and took off his belt. He emptied his pockets and placed everything into a clear plastic container and slid it down the conveyor belt and towards the x-ray machine. He walked through the large, gray metal detector and waited for the clear plastic container to make its way through the x-ray machine and to the far end of the conveyor belt.

From the surveillance video, Garcia was able to see that this person wasn't subjected to a secondary screening with one of the handheld metal detectors. This meant the original metal detector hadn't alerted the officers to the presence of any metal objects.

The clear plastic container reached the end of the conveyor belt, and the suspect placed his personal belongings back inside his pockets. He casually strolled through the silver turnstiles and was now inside the government center.

There were several people behind the first suspect and they all waited their turn to enter the government center. Garcia recognized several of the local defense attorneys and even several people he had previously arrested.

The defense attorneys all went through this same procedure every morning when they arrived at the government center. They were usually carrying large briefcases and sometimes wore long business coats. The briefcases were placed onto the conveyor belt and sent through the x-ray machine. Some of them were too large to fit through the x-ray machines and had to be examined by an officer with a handheld metal detector.

Terror from Within

The court security officers often became somewhat friendly with the defense attorneys and occasionally let them through a separate line. This allowed the attorneys special privileges without having to subject themselves to the normal security procedures during peak times at the security entrances.

The second suspect approached the north entrance to the government center just behind several defense attorneys. He was also wearing a baseball hat and walking alone. Two of the defense attorneys appeared to be talking and laughing and didn't seem to sense there was anything suspicious about the suspect who was walking in the doors right behind them. His actions mimicked that of the first suspect, and he placed his personal belongings inside of the clear plastic container and finished the rest of the screening procedures. The suspect kept scanning the entire area in and around the entrance. He didn't appear to be nervous, but his natural instincts kept him aware of what was going on around him. This type of action was indicative of some sort of prior military or law enforcement training. This suspect wasn't going to allow anything to go unnoticed, as it could have compromised the entire operation he was about to undertake. As with the first suspect, the second suspect didn't alert the court security officers that anything was suspicious.

Just as the second suspect was leaving the north entrance's security screening area, the final two suspects arrived at the south entrance to the government center. They were talking together as they approached the exterior doors. The taller of the two suspects was carrying a brown briefcase in his left hand. The other suspect was empty handed and seemed to be concentrating on what his partner was saying.

From Garcia's formal training in law enforcement, he was taught the many characteristics associated with suspicious behavior, and so far, these suspects raised minimal signs that something suspicious was occurring. The only sign was the fact that it was mid June, and with the temperature hovering in the mid-seventies, it wasn't normal for someone to be wearing any sort of bulky jacket.

Garcia's eyes returned to the first monitor in time to see the first suspect climb the stairs towards the second floor. The suspect reached the second floor and went directly into the men's restroom, which was straight across the hall from the stairway.

Garcia remembered that restroom was a single bathroom that only had one urinal and one regular toilet. In the corner was a single porcelain sink, and there would have been some sort of trash receptacle in the bathroom as well.

Meanwhile, the second suspect had entered the men's restroom located on the first floor near the circuit clerk's office. This restroom contained two bathroom stalls and a single urinal. There was a double sink in the bathroom, and the trash receptacles were built into the sink.

The first suspect exited the restroom a minute later and wiped his hands on his pants. He paused for a second just outside of the door and then walked towards the bank of elevators that were situated near the stairs.

The hallways were bustling with people as everyone was rushing to make it into court on time. The government center was originally built in 1990, and an addition

Terror from Within

was added in 2003. With the population of the county rising to approximately 200,000 people, the government center had changed dramatically within the past ten years. The recent spike in population allowed the 53rd District Court two more judges to preside over the ever-expanding court call.

The first suspect had pressed a clear button between the two elevators, and the light could be seen indicating the elevator was traveling down from the third floor. A second later, the doors to the right elevator slid open and the suspect entered the elevator along with a couple more people. The doors slid shut, and the numbers above the elevators lit up, showing the elevator had arrived at the first floor.

Chief Betts was keeping up with the suspects by pulling up each corresponding surveillance camera as the suspects moved about the government center.

The first suspect had now exited the elevator on the first floor and started towards courtroom A101.

Garcia could see that the first suspect was now walking with a noticeable limp. It was pretty obvious that this suspect was favoring his right side as he slowly made his way through the atrium and down the hallway towards courtroom A101. He kept his right arm pressed tightly against his side, and Garcia could only assume he was making sure the sawed-off assault rifle didn't raise any concerns as he approached the doors to the courtroom. Another person was just ahead of the first suspect and held the door for him as they both entered the courtroom.

The door to the courtroom closed behind them, and Garcia turned to look back at the camera showing the hallway and restroom on the first floor where the second suspect had entered. An elderly gentleman could be seen walking down the hallway past the circuit clerk's office towards the restroom. He paused at the drinking fountain, which was situated between the men's and women's restrooms, and took a sip of water. The elderly gentleman then wiped his mouth with his shirt sleeve and reached for the restroom door. He pushed the door several times and it wouldn't open. The man stood puzzled for a second and looked around, presumably to see if he missed any restroom closed signs. After seeing no signs, the man turned around and walked slowly towards the main entrance.

The elderly gentleman had walked about fifteen feet when the men's restroom door quickly opened, and the second suspect emerged. The second suspect looked both ways down the hallway before walking with a new, noticeable limp. He continued past the entrance to the government center and towards courtroom A101. He weaved his way through the maze of people stopped in front of a row of television screens as the morning's court call scrolled on each screen. He reached up with his left hand and pulled his hat down lower on his head. He kept his right arm pressed against his body during the walk to the courtroom.

He passed a long line of people who were waiting to enter courtroom A102. There was a row of chairs positioned against the opposite wall, and children were jumping around on the chairs as if it was a jungle gym.

Behind the children were large picture windows that faced the north parking lot of the government center.

The second suspect reached the door to courtroom A101 and he pulled on the handle with his left hand. The door opened, and he held the door for the lady behind him as they both entered the courtroom.

Since the south entrance of the building was higher than the north entrance, they had entered on the second floor. Garcia could see the third and fourth suspects walking side by side down the long, tiled hallway on the second floor.

There were numerous paintings on the vast white walls. Many of the area elementary schools completed art projects throughout the school year and submitted them in contests at the government center. These pieces of art were then hung on the walls for the entire community to see.

The suspects passed several doorways that led to various departments within the court system, including probation and juvenile court services. They reached the main stairs and walked down to the first floor. Once they reached the first floor, they turned to their right and walked past the main entrance for the north side of the building. They passed the row of televisions that showed the morning court call and proceeded towards courtroom A101. By now, courtroom A101 had been unlocked, and the crowd in the hallway had dissipated. There were still several people sitting quietly in the row of chairs that backed up to the big picture windows.

The last two suspects passed courtroom A101 and continued to the end of the hallway. They seemed to be checking everything out as they neared the restroom by the emergency exit. They entered the men's restroom, and the door shut behind them.

Garcia continued watching the monitor and exclaimed, "I didn't know there was a restroom near that emergency exit. Is that restroom any different that the other two bathrooms we saw the other suspects enter?"

"I don't believe so. I can't recall being in that restroom in quite a while," Chief Betts said.

A few minutes later, the door to the restroom opened and the suspects walked back down the hallway towards courtroom A101. Their heads were on swivels as they seemed to look under every chair and at every person seated near the courtrooms.

As they neared the entrance to courtroom A101, a blond woman exited the courtroom and held the door for them as they turned to the left and entered the courtroom.

Garcia wished someone would have picked up on this suspicious activity because they could have possibly alerted Bailiff Thompson and the rest of the court security division before anything could happen. With hindsight always being 20/20, it was easy to second guess the entire sequence of events he had just watched unfold on the monitors in front of him.

Chapter 12

Blake placed the cell phone he recovered from the jail cell into an electrostatic evidence bag to be logged in as evidence.

He continued searching the rest of the jail cell, carefully re-examining the bed frames to make sure there wasn't any other contraband hidden inside. All of the security locks on the electrical outlets were still in place. The ceiling lights weren't accessible to the inmates because the ceilings were too high and there wasn't any items in the cell an inmate could stand on to reach the lights.

The escaped prisoner had shared his jail cell with three other inmates. All three had been transferred to separate cells to await being interviewed by detectives. In this close space, there was a good chance one of the other inmates had heard or witnessed something suspicious about the escaped prisoner. Blake took one last look around, grabbed the evidence bag, and exited the cell. He walked back across the balcony, reached the steel-grated staircase, and slowly walked down the steps. The prisoners were still in their jail cells, and the main concourse of the cellblock was completely empty.

There were a handful of steel tables and chairs bolted to the floor and spread out amongst the main floor of the cellblock. This was the common area where the prisoners would watch television, play card games, and read books.

The correctional facility was kept at a rather cool sixty-three degrees to help eliminate the spread of bacteria or illness, which helped explain the pile of orange blankets that sat in the far corner.

Two televisions were stationed in the far corners and, for the time being, they were shut off. It was up to the correctional officers what television channels the prisoners were allowed to watch throughout the day. The prisoners didn't have the ability to change the channels when they wanted.

Since this was a county correctional facility, there wasn't any outside exercise time for the inmates. They spent twenty-four hours a day locked up inside the confines of the cement-block walls.

The correctional officers usually became dependant on the inmates to keep the operations of each cellblock running smoothly. There was always a give and take between the inmates and the correctional officers. Some inmates would keep an eye out for trouble and contraband and pass the word along to the officers. In turn, the officers would provide the snitches with extra treats when the commissary came around. If an inmate was able to provide more valuable information beyond the small things occurring in the jail, he could speak with a detective from the sheriff's office and try to work a plea deal for his own case.

Blake arrived at the steel door located at the far end of the cellblock. He pressed the button on the intercom system and waited to be buzzed through the door.

Terror from Within

"Do you need help carrying anything?" a female voice said through the speaker located next to the intercom button.

"I'm all set," Blake said, glancing back across the cellblock.

A few seconds later, a buzzing noise could be heard coming from the door, and Blake was able to push the heavy door outward. He stepped into a hallway, and the door shut behind him.

The sergeant, who had brought him up to cellblock seven, was standing near a computer located behind the counter. She finished her conversation with the other correctional officer and then escorted Blake back downstairs to the lobby.

Blake thanked her for the assistance and left out the front door of the jail. He walked across the front courtyard and approached the main lobby of the courthouse. He showed his badge to the court security officers who were stationed at the entrance. One of them nodded and pointed for him to enter through the metal detectors.

Blake looked to the left as he walked through the metal detectors, which made a loud beeping noise as he passed through them. He approached Sheriff Calhoun and Chief Ed Kowalski of corrections, who were talking at a small, round table in the corner of the atrium.

"Sorry to interrupt, but something very urgent has come up," Blake said quietly, pulling a chair away from the table. He took a seat and showed them the photographs from inside the jail cell.

Both of their mouths dropped open as Blake showed them the photograph depicting the cellular phone hidden inside the bed frame. Chief Kowalski's face quickly became a flush red; Sheriff Calhoun looked over at him with a quizzical look.

The correctional facility employed over three hundred officers and Chief Kowalski knew it was going to be next to impossible to track down how the cellular phone entered the jail. He always prided himself on providing great security and keeping the morale high among the correctional officers.

"This breach of security is going to be my first priority," Chief Kowalski stammered as his mind spun. "We need to make sure there aren't more attacks being planned using this sort of communication."

"Could you please send the escaped prisoner's cellmates up to the detective bureau, one at a time?" Blake whispered. "I need to make sure there wasn't an insider who provided this cell phone to the inmate."

"I'll make sure I have a lieutenant personally take each prisoner up for questioning. I don't want anyone with frequent inmate contact to be bringing these inmates up to you."

"We would greatly appreciate that," the sheriff said as he looked the chief in the eyes. "We hate to compromise the investigation by letting this piece of information get to the correctional officers."

"I'll head up to our office and get an interview room ready," Blake explained as he stood up from the chair.

The chief looked up at Blake and said, "I'll have the first inmate brought up within ten minutes."

Blake thanked them both for their time and left the atrium. He glanced down at his watch as he walked down the tiled hallway and up the first flight of stairs. It was almost 2:30 p.m., and there was still so much of this investigation that needed to be completed before anyone could think about going home to get some sleep.

He reached the detective bureau and opened the door. The division had mostly cleared out since the interviews of witnesses had wrapped up. He went into the audio/visual (AV) room and started up the recording system for the first interview.

He quickly stopped at the bathroom and relieved himself before returning to his office. Blake pulled out his cell phone and called his wife. He gave her a brief synopsis of the day's events and told her he had no idea when he'd be done for the day. He asked how the children were doing and hit the end button before Maria could voice her opinion about when he'd return home.

Blake looked over at the telephone in his office just as it began to ring. He picked up the receiver and listened as a lieutenant from the corrections division told him they were waiting outside the detective bureau.

Blake walked down the carpeted hallway and went to the main entrance of the bureau. The entrance of the investigations division contained a small waiting area with several brown plastic chairs. A small magazine rack sat in the corner and held several outdated magazines. A bulletproof pane of glass separated the waiting area from the receptionist who usually staffed the desk during normal business hours.

He opened the door to let the lieutenant and inmate into the office. He walked them down the hallway and told the inmate to sit in the first interview room. After the inmate took a seat, Blake said he'd be right back and then he pulled the door shut.

The lieutenant was dressed in his normal black BDUs and black shirt. His boots were well shined and his pants appeared to have been recently pressed.

He handed Blake a note card indicating who the inmate was and why he was being held in the jail. Blake asked, "Can you keep an eye on the inmate via the monitor in the AV room? I'm going to do a quick background check on the inmate."

Blake searched all previous arrests and contacts for the inmate. He didn't appear to have any association with the escaped prisoner. He was being held on numerous drug charges and was known to be uncooperative with the police.

Blake secured his firearm into a gun locker and entered the interview room. The inmate was staring intently at the wall, and his gaze turned to Blake as he entered the room. He was dressed in the normal orange jumpsuit and Crocs. His hair was long, uncombed, and greasy. His face was narrow, and a small scar was located on his right cheek.

Blake hadn't had the pleasure of dealing with this individual in the past, but his name was common around the law enforcement circles. He was known for breaking into places and stealing anything he could get his hands on to help support his heroin habit. He had been in and out of the court system since he was eighteen years old, and he probably knew more about the criminal justice system than any veteran police officer would ever know in his or her career. He knew his rights and ways to manipulate the system in his favor.

Terror from Within

"I'm guessing you know why you're being brought up here today," Blake began, sitting down at the table across from the inmate.

"I ain't going to help you with anything," he said as he looked defiantly at Blake. "All you cops are the same, you never follow through with your promises."

"Let me just explain a few things to you and after I'm done, maybe we can still talk."

"I still ain't sayin' shit, but if you want to waste your breath, then go right ahead."

Blake read the inmate his Miranda warnings and then filled him in on the details of the morning's escape. Blake told him about searching his jail cell and finding a cellular phone in a hollowed-out portion of the bed frame.

"I know you're aware of the cell phone and I'm looking to work out a deal for your most recent case," Blake said, looking over at the inmate. "I've never had to deal with you before and I'm not about to screw around. If I promise you something, I'll make sure it's taken care of. I need to know how that cellular phone got into the jail and what kinds of phone calls were made from it."

"I don't know shit about no cell phone," the inmate stated, looking down at the brown table. "I didn't use no cell phone and I didn't see no cell phone."

"We're not looking to get you in trouble if you happened to talk on the cell phone. I need to know how it got into the jail and whom the escaped inmate may have been talking to. I'm positive the state's attorney's office will work a plea deal with you if you have any information about this cell phone."

"What kind of deal are you talking about? Because I ain't saying nothin' until I can get a guarantee in writing. So, until you can promise me that, you're just wasting your time."

"I can't promise you anything because I'm not the one who negotiates cases. It would be up to the state's attorney's office and the judge on what kind of deal they could work out with you. Until you give me some details on what you know, I won't be able to speak to the SA's office and let them know you're assisting us with this investigation."

"You don't want to hear what I'm going to say about that cell phone," the inmate continued, confidently sitting back in his chair and crossing his arms. "I ain't going to bullshit you. I've done a few licks in my past and I got caught. Now I'm ready to turn my life around and try to get a real job. I just got my GED and I've been looking for a job, but it's tough out there with this economy. I just got married to my girl, and we're looking for a place to live."

"Do you have any kids?" Blake said, trying to make small talk.

"I have another baby momma, but she lives in Texas and she never lets me see my son. I really want to move down there with my girl so I can see my son on a regular basis, but my baby momma wouldn't let me."

"Well, here's a chance to turn your life around and provide us with some potentially useful information as you try to straighten your life around."

"I just need to get away from this county and start over with a clean record."

Terror from Within

"Do you smoke?" Blake asked, flipping through his stack of paperwork.

"Yeah," the inmate replied, his eyes perking up. "Man, I haven't had a cigarette in over a month."

"Sit tight for a minute, and I'll get you a smoke," Blake said, standing up from the chair and grabbing his pile of paperwork.

Blake went into the main office and opened up one of the cupboards. They always kept a carton of Newport cigarettes in the office just in case they needed a little incentive for an inmate. He grabbed a pack of cigarettes out of the carton and pulled out a single cigarette. He grabbed a lighter from inside of the cupboard.

Blake walked back to the interview room and gave the inmate a cigarette, sliding an ashtray across the table. He lit the cigarette and then let the inmate finish the cigarette before leaving the interview room.

Blake returned to his office and made a telephone call to the SA's office. He spoke with a felony review SA who looked up the inmate's court cases. After reviewing the file, the SA advised Blake that he wasn't willing to work any plea deals with this inmate. "He's been arrested too many times for burglary and drug charges."

Blake tried to explain that this escaped prisoner was a higher priority than a simple drug charge, but the SA didn't want to hear anything about it.

Blake slammed the phone down onto its cradle and shouted, "What a worthless piece of shit! I can't believe this guy."

He pulled out his cell phone and called Sheriff Calhoun directly. He explained the situation to the sheriff and how the SA's office wasn't willing to assist with this case. Blake hated going over someone's head, but he wasn't going to let some know-it-all SA stop him from potentially breaking this case wide open. The sheriff thanked him for the phone call and told him he'd call the head of the SA's office to have this issue straightened out.

A few minutes later, Blake's cellular phone rang. He glanced at the caller ID long enough to see it was the sheriff calling back. He flipped the phone open and pressed it to his ear.

The sheriff explained how he had twisted the state's attorney's arm, and they were willing to assist the sheriff's office with a plea deal if the inmate could provide useful information.

Blake returned to the interview room and filled the inmate in on the details of a plea agreement if he could provide information useful to the escape.

"I know about the cell phone being in our cell. I personally used it on several occasions to call my girl," he said "The guy who escaped was the one who had it brought into the jail. He never told us how he got it, but there has been some chatter around our cellblock."

Blake wasn't taking notes as the inmate continued with his statement. He was making mental notes and would be able to review the recording of the interview later.

"Many of us feel that guy had a more personal relationship with one of the female correctional officers up in that cellblock. That female officer had brought him down to several of his court dates, and he told some of us afterwards that they had a thing goin' on between them. He never said what it was, other than he had something goin' on with her. I feel that he may have provided her with some sort of sexual gratification, and in return she felt the need to provide him with a cell phone, so he wouldn't squeal on her."

∽∾

The SWAT team filed in through the open glass door of the rest stop building. Once inside the building, the team was split equally on each side of the vestibule. Each side of the vestibule had two steel doors at the far end and one steel door closest to the SWAT team.

They proceeded to walk in a single stack along the wall until each line reached its respective doors. The first deputy passed the doorway and kept his AR-15 trained towards the doorways on the far side of the lobby. The second deputy in the stack walked past the closed door and positioned himself below the first officer to assist with covering the far doors.

The third deputy signaled to the rest of the stack that he was going to be checking the door just as he reached for the door handle. He attempted to turn the knob, but it was locked. Another signal was given, and both stacks moved forward to allow the rest of their men to go past the first set of locked doors.

The two rear deputies took up a rear guard and kept their eyes on the first locked door as the rest of the team continued towards the far set of doors.

On the left side of the lobby, there was a sign indicating the entrance to the men's restroom, and a similar sign indicated the entrance to the ladies restroom on the right side of the lobby.

As both stacks continued forward, the door on the far right side of the lobby started to open. The deputies who were standing across the lobby immediately trained their assault rifles on the door as it continued opening.

Chapter 13

"Can you pause the video for a second? I need to use the restroom," Garcia said, standing up from his swivel chair.

Chief Betts clicked the left button on the mouse, and the computer screen stopped. "I'll rewind the surveillance video so we can see who may have visited the restrooms prior to our suspects," the chief added.

Garcia walked to the back of the room and opened the door to a private restroom reserved for the court security officers. He shut the door and walked over to the urinal. He relieved himself and then zipped his pants back up. He turned away from the urinal, and it flushed automatically. He stepped up to the sink and placed his hand under the soap dispenser; a bluish foam squirted out of the bottom. He placed his left hand under the faucet and a stream of water automatically started flowing towards the drain.

He continued washing his hands, staring blankly at the mirror. He wasn't looking at anything in particular when he heard a muffled rumbling sound coming from someplace in the building. The floor shook, and Garcia heard things in the surveillance room crash to the floor.

He bolted out of the restroom without pausing to dry his hands. Chief Betts was staring at the row of monitors with a blank look on his face. He pointed to the monitor on the far left. Piles of broken cement blocks and dust filled the screen.

"What in the hell was that?" Garcia said, his voice quivering slightly.

"Holy shit—I was watching this surveillance camera when a large blast blew out the entire block wall of the restroom where all of the investigators were processing the scene," Chief Betts said, a bewildered look on his face.

Garcia watched the monitor, which showed a view from a surveillance camera positioned father down the hallway from the blast; he could see several police officers rushing towards the debris.

Chief Betts's Motorola radio immediately crackled to life.

"Help! Get this shit off me," someone frantically screamed over the radio, obviously trapped inside the rubble.

Paramedics rushed gurneys towards the blast site. Within minutes, the area around the blast was swarming with rescue personnel.

A call was heard over their portable radios, indicating that the fire department was responding with their building collapse specialists. They had enough technical equipment to effectively sift through the rubble to search for anyone who happened to be trapped by debris.

Chief Betts made the decision that they would stay in the surveillance command center to keep an eye out for any other suspicious activity going on around the government center.

Garcia's thoughts drifted back to his days at the police academy. One of their blocks of instruction was on terrorists and their methods of attacks. Garcia distinctly remembered hearing the instructor speak about secondary explosions. These explosions were designed to injure and kill responding investigators.

Garcia started to shake ever so slightly. He was never one to back down from the dangers of police work, and up until today he was always calm and collected during the most stressful police calls. The thoughts of a terrorist attack in this little suburban town caught him by complete surprise.

On Sept. 11th, 2001, terrorists attacked Americans in and around New York City and Washington, D.C. Afterwards, there was a tremendous outpouring of support for the areas devastated by the attacks. The thought of someone actually attacking Humble County was something that had never even crossed his mind.

Garcia couldn't remember receiving any terrorism training outside of the police academy. The Department of Homeland Security hadn't provided the local police agencies with any formal terrorism training. He remembered a generic index card that was distributed one day at roll call, but no federal agency ever came into the county to keep the local police up to date on any issues that could have been brewing in their area.

The Humble County Sheriff's Office didn't have the resources to maintain its own database on terrorism threats. It wasn't practical for them to have their own organized crime division, as they were hardly able to staff enough deputies to respond to normal calls for service.

Garcia watched the fire fighters and paramedics enter the cloud of dust that surrounded the rubble. The fire fighters were using their SCBAs to assist with breathing because the dust cloud limited the visibility to under a foot.

Chief Betts couldn't take his eyes off the surveillance monitors. "I remember hearing about secondary explosive devices several years ago during one of those abortion clinic bombings. I'm going to check with the sheriff to see if he wants us to expand the crime scene to include a greater area around the government center."

The chief picked up his cell phone and hit the speed dial button for Sheriff Calhoun. After a brief pause, Chief Betts said, "Sir, I know you're busy, but I wanted to see if we could expand the crime scene to several hundred yards outside of the government center property. I would hate for there to be another explosive device sitting in the parking lot and cause more casualties than we already have."

The chief nodded his head in agreement as he listened to the sheriff's response. He thanked the sheriff for his time and then slid his cell phone closed.

"All off-duty members of the sheriff's office were notified to respond to the government center right away. They will be setting up a secondary staging area at Buckley Middle School across the street. The patrol deputies are evacuating the news media from the parking lot and making them set up farther down the road. The sheriff has been in contact with the ATF along with the FBI. Both agencies have investigators en route to the government center as we speak." The chief shook his head in disbelief.

"That's exactly what we need. A bunch of federal jackasses who think their shit doesn't stink. Why is it that these guys are never around until a major incident strikes? I haven't seen one of their agents stop in the office to see how things are going or to share intelligence since I've been in the bureau. Now they are all going to show up with their acronym-filled jackets and push their weight around," Garcia said, his face flushed red. He could feel his heart racing as he tightly clenched his fists.

"I understand your point. I spent all these years in law enforcement and I never saw the feds take any case unless it would make big headline news. I hate to say this, but I really think we're going to need their assistance with this investigation. They have the equipment and training necessary to investigate this explosion. Our arson investigators just don't have the training to fully investigate the origin and cause of the explosion. We'll have to rely on their training to fully investigate what is arguably the biggest terrorism incident to occur in Michigan," the chief said, looking over the top of his glasses.

Garcia knew the chief was right but didn't want to let on that this case was way over their heads. He knew the sheriff's office was good at investigating burglaries, robberies, and even homicides, for that matter. The problem was this attack surely had ties that would extend far beyond the boundaries of the county. To Garcia's knowledge, there weren't any extremist groups active in the county. There was always a chance a sleeper cell was operating within the county, but why would an inmate without any known ties to extremist groups all of a sudden show up on the radar in such a catastrophic manner?

These questions, along with many others, would probably be answered someday, but that day wasn't going to come soon enough for the citizens of Humble County.

Chapter 14

Blake's thoughts were running rampant as he finished interviewing the first inmate. He couldn't help but assume the worst from his conversation with this inmate. Not only had the inmate indicated a possible personal relationship between the now-escaped inmate and a female correctional officer, but he had also told Blake about the female providing him with special privileges.

The escaped inmate was allowed more time to roam the cellblock than the other inmates. When this particular female correctional officer was working in his block, the inmate wasn't subject to the same quiet-time rules as everyone else.

This investigation was going from bad to worse in a matter of minutes. The correctional officer would have to be identified and then brought in for questioning.

Blake stepped out of the interview room and signaled to the lieutenant that he was done with the interview of the first inmate.

The lieutenant escorted the inmate out of the interview room, and Blake walked them out of the detective bureau.

Blake returned to the A/V room and stopped the recording of the first interview. He pushed the eject button on the DVR system, and the drawer slid open. He grabbed the DVD off the tray and placed it into an evidence envelope. He labeled the envelope with the appropriate inmate's name and included the date and time of the interview.

Blake placed a new DVD into the tray and pressed the eject button to close the drawer.

He then returned to his office and sat down in his black swivel chair. He picked up the receiver on his office phone and placed a call to Detective Sergeant McGuire. Blake briefed McGuire on the events of the first interview. Blake requested to have a supervisor respond to the investigations division to assist with the other two inmate interviews. Just as he was about to hang up the phone, he felt the building shake from the explosion on the first floor.

"Oh, shit, that didn't sound good," Blake yelled into the phone.

"What happened?"

"There was just a loud boom and the building shook. I'll have to make my way downstairs to see what's going on."

"I'm heading over that way right now. Be safe and keep me updated."

With that, Blake hung up the phone. He quickly dialed the number to the court security surveillance office.

Chief Betts answered the phone and quickly filled Blake in on what he saw on the surveillance monitors. He informed Blake he would be staying in the surveillance room to keep an eye on the rest of the government center.

Terror from Within

Blake picked up his cell phone and dialed Sergeant McGuire's phone number. After the phone rang three times, he heard a voice on the other end.

"Hello?"

"There was an explosion on the first floor of the government center. I just spoke with Chief Betts, and he thinks it was a secondary device used to kill investigators who were in the area after the initial escape. Chief Betts said the entire area around the emergency exit was destroyed in the blast. He said there are enough first responders on scene and, as much as I hate to be missing out on the action, I'm going to stay up in the office and finish up these interviews. We need to gather this intelligence as quickly as possible."

"I agree; we all need to be doing our part to get this case resolved as quickly as possible. I'm heading over there right now and I'll help out with the interviews."

Blake hung up the phone and began a background check on the second and third inmates. Neither of them had a connection to the now-escaped inmate, and they were currently being held on unrelated charges.

Blake had called the sergeant to provide another set of eyes for the interviews and to get the ball rolling for an upcoming internal investigation in the corrections division.

Fifteen minutes later, Blake heard the door open at the front of the office and Detective Sergeant McGuire could be heard walking down the hallway. He entered Blake's office and sat down in a plain, black-cushioned chair.

Detective Sergeant McGuire had worked his entire career with the sheriff's office. He had been hired as a road patrol deputy in 1981, had served on the SWAT team, and was an accident investigator. He was assigned to the detective bureau in 1993. He attended an interview and interrogation class shortly after being assigned to the bureau and was soon considered a master in this field. The training provided tremendous insight into the reasons or motivations for people to commit crimes and allowed Sergeant McGuire to quickly determine if someone was being deceitful.

McGuire had a worried look on his face and Blake could tell the earlier events were starting to take an emotional toll on him.

"The second inmate should be arriving shortly," Blake said, looking over at Sergeant McGuire.

"Blake, this day can't end soon enough. I have a gut feeling that this investigation is going to get a lot worse before it gets better. Lieutenant Young called me a little while ago to inform me they located the green van at the interstate rest stop just east of Three Forks."

Sergeant McGuire paused just long enough for Blake to ask a question. "Based on your demeanor, I'm guessing that the suspects had already fled the area?" Blake interjected.

"Well, that hasn't exactly been determined yet. The SWAT team has the building completely surrounded and they are attempting to make contact with someone on the inside."

"These suspects are way too sophisticated to stick around and use the bathroom at the rest stop. I'm sure they are long gone."

"You may be right, but until the building has been searched, we can't rule out that possibility. A trooper found the van fully engulfed in flames at the back of the parking lot. They've sent out a helicopter to search the area in case the suspects fled through the wooded area behind the rest stop."

As Sergeant McGuire finished his sentence, the doorbell rang, signaling the arrival of the second inmate.

The second inmate was led to an interview room and took a seat next to the table. Blake started the video recorder for the interview room and then entered the room with Sergeant McGuire.

Blake asked the second inmate the same series of questions as he asked the first inmate. The results of this interview were similar to the statements of the first inmate. They both figured the female corrections officer was somehow involved in providing a cell phone for them to use.

Blake thanked the second inmate for being cooperative and released him back into the custody of the lieutenant from the corrections division.

The third inmate was brought in for questioning, and he denied having any knowledge of the cell phone or knowing anything about a possible relationship between the now escaped inmate and any corrections officers.

After the third interview was completed, Sergeant McGuire called Lieutenant Young and filled him in on the status of the interviews. The consensus was that

Chief Kowalski would be contacted and filled in on the new information. The chief would have to decide how the information would be disseminated throughout the corrections division. One thing was for certain, they couldn't trust anyone until the female correctional officer was identified.

Sergeant McGuire picked up the phone and dialed the chief's cell phone number, which he now knew by memory. He asked the chief to meet him in the detective bureau and he'd fill him in on the details of the inmate interviews. Chief Kowalski told Sergeant McGuire that he would retrieve his laptop computer from his office and then walk over to the detective bureau. Chief Kowalski told Sergeant McGuire he would search his database to narrow down the female correctional officer the inmates had talked about.

Sergeant McGuire and Blake sat down in the conference room and began dissecting the events from earlier in the day.

"We need to find out who the escaped inmate was connected to because this sort of assault on the government center isn't something your average citizen is going to be able to pull off," Sergeant McGuire said, staring across the room in the direction of the white erase board.

"I wish we had a system that could track known associates and give us some sort of lead into where this guy may be headed," Blake thought aloud.

The sheriff's department was in the process of going through a computer database change and this sort of information wasn't available because of the new system's limitations. The Emergency Management Agency was the main proponent of the changes and never received advice from the police officers and detectives who used this sort of program on a daily basis. The bids went out for a record management system, and the bid went to the cheapest vendor without regard for its functionality in the real world.

Blake had run into this sort of problem ever since he began working for the sheriff's department in 2000. There were always new technological changes coming and going in this line of work, and not every new system offered something useful to the sheriff's office.

They continued tossing around potential connections between the escaped inmate and several organized criminal groups. The sheriff's office didn't have the resources to gain useful intelligence on these groups. The FBI never attended the regular intelligence meetings in the area and rarely sent out intelligence information from their organized crime division. This lack of information sharing left the local agencies in the dark when it came to the details and resources available to some of these more advanced organized criminal groups.

The doorbell to the front door of the detective bureau pierced the silence and Blake sprang to his feet. He walked down the hallway at a fast pace and reached the entrance to the investigations bureau within a few seconds. Blake opened the door leading into the waiting area and welcomed Chief Kowalski into the office.

"Thanks for getting up here so quickly," Blake said as he led the chief down the hallway and into the conference room.

"Not a problem at all. We're all in this mess together, and I appreciate the open communication," the chief replied.

"Chief, we've just finished interviewing the three inmates who share a cell with the inmate who escaped," Sergeant McGuire began.

He filled the chief in on the details of the interviews. When he was finished, Sergeant McGuire looked up from his notepad.

"Chief, you know as well as I do that we need to keep a lid on this investigation. If any word leaks out about this issue, it will compromise any future interviews," Sergeant McGuire said.

"Let me sign into my computer and I'll be able to search which correctional officers have had contact with the escaped inmate. I'll be able to look up who transported him to and from his jail cell each time. Then we can review the surveillance video from the jail to match up any accusations."

The chief pecked away at his computer and soon he had opened the database that allowed him to search each inmate's movement throughout the jail. He typed in the name of the inmate and hit the enter button. A new page loaded on the computer screen and it showed the complete list of the inmate's whereabouts since he had been arrested. The list also detailed every place the inmate was brought while being incarcerated in the jail.

All three looked over the list and Blake wrote down the names of the female correctional officers who had transported the inmate to or from a court date.

Terror from Within

The jail had a standing policy that discouraged members of the opposite sex from transporting an inmate to or from a court date. So, after searching the entire list, they were down to only two females who had transported the inmate within the jail.

Blake arranged two separate six-person photo lineups to present to the inmates they had interviewed. In each photo lineup, he included one of the female correctional officers who had transported the inmate within the jail.

Neither of the two officers had any previous reprimands while employed with the sheriff's department. This further complicated the potential breach of security within the department.

Chief Kowalski used his department-issued cell phone and contacted the lieutenant who had previously brought the inmates up for questioning. The chief advised him to bring the first inmate up right away.

The inmate arrived within fifteen minutes and was placed in an interview room. Blake and McGuire entered the room with a stack of paperwork.

Blake read the inmate a form that described the way the photo lineup would be conducted. He informed the inmate that the correctional officer in question may or may not be included in the photo lineup. Blake also informed the inmate he wasn't obligated to select anyone if he didn't recognize any of the people in the lineup.

The inmate agreed to the procedure and signed the acknowledgment.

Blake slid the first six-person photo lineup across the table and placed it in front of the inmate. The inmate

Craig L'Esperance

glanced at the photographs sitting before him and immediately pointed to photograph number three.

"That's her right there," the inmate said confidently.

"Where have you seen her before?" Blake asked.

"She's the one who everyone suspects of bringing in the cell phone."

"Okay, if you could please circle her photograph and put your initials next to it," Blake said, reaching for the second photo lineup.

After the inmate circled the photo and placed his initials next to it, Blake placed the first photo lineup back into his stack of papers. Then he slid the second photo lineup in front of the inmate.

"She's not in this photo lineup," the inmate said, after he looked over the photographs.

Blake took the second photo lineup and placed it into his stack of paperwork.

"Thanks again for your cooperation. I'll let you know if this information works out."

With that, Blake stood up and opened the door to the interview room. The inmate stood up and followed Blake out of the room. Blake turned the inmate over to the lieutenant, who was sitting in the waiting room.

Ten minutes later, the lieutenant brought the second inmate back up to the detective bureau. Blake administered the first photo lineups to this inmate.

"She is the one whom we all suspect of having a relationship with that guy who escaped," the inmate said positively.

"Have you seen her anywhere other than at the jail?" Blake asked.

Terror from Within

"No, I've only been in the jail for two weeks. I've never seen her before being arrested and placed in block seven."

"Could you please circle her photograph and put your initials inside of the circle?"

The inmate followed the instructions and placed the pen onto the table.

"What are the chances that I'll be able to bond out soon?" he asked.

"I'll be in contact with the SA's office as soon as I have a chance to verify what you're telling me. I really appreciate you talking with us and I'll keep you posted."

Blake stood up and opened the door to the interview room. He motioned for the inmate to stand up and follow him back down the hallway towards the waiting room. Blake turned the inmate back over to the lieutenant, who was reading a year-old edition of *Golf Digest*.

With the two inmates picking the same female correctional officer out of the photo lineups, Blake was confident they had the right person to interview.

Blake and McGuire returned to the conference room.

Chief Kowalski exited the AV room and walked down the hallway and into the conference room. From the look on his face, Blake could tell the chief had been watching the administration of the photo lineup via the AV room.

The accusation of the cell phone being brought into the jail by a female corrections officer wasn't going to sit well with the sheriff. The sheriff's office had already failed to provide a secure facility where the democratic government could run smoothly without any interruptions. Now, the possibility of an insider assisting an inmate was slowly being uncovered.

McGuire, Kowalski, and Blake discussed ideas on how they could determine if the female correctional officer had actually brought the cell phone in for the inmates.

They knew that a high-tech surveillance system monitored and recorded each entrance to the correctional facility. Most spots in and around the jail were also monitored by audio and video surveillance. The only problem was there were several dead zones that weren't covered by any sort of surveillance. It was common knowledge with the correctional officers where each and every dead zone was in case an emergency developed in those areas.

With that said, the female correctional officer would know where she could provide an inmate with a cell phone without it being recorded. One of the main areas where this could occur would be en route from the jail to the courtrooms.

Blake returned to the conference room and sat down in a leather executive-style chair.

"Well, it looks like we're going to have a little chat with Ms. Joanne Sullivan," Sergeant McGuire said as he leaned back in his chair.

"She happens to be working today" the chief added, scrolling through the schedule on his laptop computer. "We'll get her up here this afternoon before she has a chance to develop a story."

Chapter 15

As the door at the far end of the vestibule slowly opened, the deputies on the opposite side of the lobby could see a gray cart appear through the doorway first. The entire cart came into view just before a man in his thirties walked through the doorway.

The closest deputies quickly approached the man as he stepped completely into the lobby.

The man was wearing brown work boots, blue jeans, plaid button-up shirt, and a dark-green baseball cap. He hadn't noticed the SWAT team until the first deputies were already taking him to the ground.

The deputies didn't have time to ask the man any questions. They needed to mitigate any potential danger he posed before asking questions. The man was quickly handcuffed, and two deputies swiftly escorted him out the front door.

The remaining team members searched the entire building but didn't locate anyone else inside. The SWAT commander used his headset and called the dispatchers to advise them that the building had been cleared.

The man was interviewed on scene, and he told the deputies that he had arrived at the rest stop about an hour ago. He said his company was hired by MDOT to install energy-efficient bathroom faucets and hand dryers. He never saw the suspects arrive at the rest stop or abandon their van. The man couldn't remember how many other vehicles were in the parking lot when he had arrived.

A few detectives arrived and assisted with a secondary search of the building for any possible evidence related to the government center attack. After finding nothing of interest, the man was released to pick up his belongings. They advised him the area was being treated as a crime scene and he would have to return later to complete his work.

Detectives canvassed the area around where the van was found burning. The area had been saturated with water during the firefighting efforts, and any potential evidence was consumed in the intense heat from inside of the burning van.

The search was expanded to include the wooded area around the rest stop. A MSP helicopter flew back and forth over the area, trying to pick up any trace of the suspects in the woods.

A plan was formulated, and the detectives walked in a straight line searching for clues until they had cleared the entire field leading up to the woods behind the rest stop. The initial canvass of the area indicated someone might have left the area through the field, as there were several spots where the long grass was trampled down.

Since the underbrush was thick in several areas, investigators decided to use the two K-9s from the sheriff's office to track the suspects.

The entire area in and around the rest stop had already been contaminated by many scents, so the K-9 deputies decided to start tracking near the tree line.

Terror from Within

One of the K-9s, Scout, alerted to a possible scent about fifty yards into the wooded area. Scout started trotting in a zigzag pattern into the woods. By this time, nearly fifty police officers had joined the search and were following behind Scout and his handler.

Scout led them through the wooded area and stopped at a clearing on the far side. It was evident that two vehicles had been hidden in the brush on the edge of the tree line. Two sets of tire impressions in the brush traveled through a small section of field before driving onto an adjacent gravel road.

Evidence technicians were called out to the area to cast the tire impression evidence. The ETs took measurements of the width between the tire impressions and photographed the area. They also were able to locate several fresh tire impressions in the muddy ditch that led up to the gravel road. The ETs used dental stone to preserve the actual tire impression so they could be sent to the crime lab for analysis.

There weren't any homes in the immediate area, and the gravel road was well isolated. The surrounding fields were full of sweet corn, and it was obvious that the suspects had left the area unnoticed.

It was 5 p.m. and the sun was still high in the sky; the sweltering heat was taking its toll on every officer in the area.

After the entire area around the gravel road was canvassed, the weary investigators trudged back to the rest stop.

The American Red Cross had sent a relief van out to the rest stop to assist the investigators with snacks and beverages. As most of the group milled around, catching a quick bite to eat, Lieutenant Young approached them from the parking lot.

"Hello, everyone. First of all, I want to thank you all for your hard work and persistence throughout today's horrific events. I wanted to make sure everyone was aware there was an explosion at the government center a short time ago."

Most of the investigators gasped at the news and focused their attention on the lieutenant.

"I want to make sure everyone goes home safe to their families, so please be careful and watch each other's backs because these bastards mean business!"

Chapter 16

Blake contacted the on-call assistant state's attorney and filled him in on how he located the cell phone inside of the jail cell. It was agreed that Blake would complete a search warrant for the phone so he could determine what the telephone number was for the phone. He completed the necessary paperwork for the search warrant and met with a judge inside of the detective bureau. The ASA and the judge left the bureau after facilitating the signing of the search warrant.

After the search warrant was signed, Blake pulled the cell phone out of the electrostatic evidence bag. He browsed through the menu options on the phone until he reached the option for phone details. There, he located the telephone number of the phone. The memory had been erased, and there weren't any text messages or recent calls. He re-secured the cell phone inside of the electrostatic evidence bag and returned it to a secure evidence locker.

Back in his office, Blake opened up his desk drawer, which contained copies of forms he used on a regular basis. He searched through the file folders and located the stack of subpoena forms. He pulled one of the forms out of the stack and placed the file folder back into the drawer. He slid the drawer closed and glanced at the subpoena form before filling it out. Blake reached over and double clicked on the Internet Explorer icon on his computer. Within a few seconds, the Google search engine popped up on the screen. He was soon logged into the department's search engine for cell phone numbers. He was able to locate the cellular phone carrier for the phone he found in the jail. There was a section that listed the carrier's subpoena contact information. Blake filled in the rest of the information on the subpoena request form and placed it on the side of his desk.

He pulled up his department e-mail account and sent an e-mail to the secretary for the SA's office who handled the scheduling for all grand jury subpoena requests. Blake needed to testify at grand jury as quickly as possible. The cellular phone providers recently began limiting the amount of information they store on their databases. It was becoming obvious that this cellular phone was the escaped prisoner's life line to the outside world.

The prisoner had used the cellular phone to circumvent the recorded jail telephone system. Without any of the inmate's phone calls being recorded, it was impossible for the investigation to determine who the inmate was speaking with unless the subpoena request turned up the required evidence.

Now it was up to the cellular phone carrier to respond to the subpoena request, and the results might not be available for two months. This crucial piece of evidence was going to have to sit on the back burner until the request came back.

Terror from Within

"I don't think this day is ever going to end," Garcia thought as he sat next to Chief Betts in the surveillance office. "I'd better let my wife know I won't be coming home anytime soon."

He reached into his left pants pocket and took his cell phone out of his pocket. Instead of calling his wife, he decided to send her a text message. He let her know there was a big incident at the government center and he would be tied up for a while. He added the fact that he was safe and he would call her when he got a chance.

The chief tried several times to reach Sheriff Calhoun through his portable radio but he didn't get any response. He tried to ping the sheriff on his Nextel, but he kept getting a busy signal.

Chief Betts picked up the telephone that was mounted to the wall and called down to the north entrance of the government center. One of the court security officers answered the phone.

"North entrance, this is Bill," a voice said.

"It's Chief Betts, What are things looking like down there?"

"Chief, it looks like a warzone down here. There were probably ten to fifteen investigators still in the area when the blast happened. At this time, we still have several investigators unaccounted for," Bill added.

"Can you tell where this blast came from?"

"I'm getting reports that the blast came from inside one of the bathrooms near the emergency exit. The exterior windows were blown out during the explosion. The entire wall that runs from courtroom A101 to the emergency exit is completely demolished. We've got piles of cinder blocks keeping us from moving any closer to the trapped officers. The Three Forks Fire Department has its technical rescue team on scene and they are just starting to remove debris piece by piece."

"Can you get the sheriff on the line for me? I need to speak with him right away."

"I'll have someone track him down and give you a call in the surveillance office," Bill said.

"Shit, you know what? I remember seeing one of those last suspects enter the courthouse with a brown briefcase. I don't recall seeing him leave the bathroom with the briefcase," Garcia said aloud. "I know those suspects went through the metal detectors, but what if the explosive wasn't detectable with the equipment at the entrances? If I would have recognized it earlier, there is a chance we could have had a bomb squad clear the hallway and restroom prior to the investigators entering the area."

"We conduct unannounced security reviews and we haven't had any issues in the past with allowing contraband into the government center. That doesn't mean something couldn't get past the system without being detected," the chief added. "We'll have to wait until the sheriff calls back to get more details on the blast. In the meantime, let's continue watching the surveillance video prior to the government center opening this morning. I have a hunch that someone had a hand in assisting these guys."

"I agree, and we still don't have an explanation for how those high- powered rifles got into the building."

The surveillance system had been upgraded in 2003 during the expansion of the government center. The one-million-dollar digital system was highly sophisticated

Terror from Within

compared to the old VHS system. All of the cameras included infrared capabilities, which allowed them to monitor areas that were under complete darkness. The cameras were programmed to only record if there was movement within their field of view. This allowed the system to store more video, since the system wasn't bogged down by saving hours of recordings from the overnight hours when the government building was unoccupied.

Chief Betts set up the surveillance system to begin at 10:00 p.m. the previous night. The government center doesn't provide around-the-clock security. Several court security officers worked the afternoon shift until 10:00 p.m. The officers had all usually vacated the building by 10:15 p.m. After the court security officers left the government center, the building would have been completely empty. The surveillance system began rolling as they continued watching the video; most of the screens remained blank. They saw the three afternoon-shift maintenance workers moving from area to area, cleaning the building. The maintenance workers all stayed in the same vicinity and it was easy to keep an eye on their movements. They closed up their office and left the building just prior to the court security officers leaving for the night, and the government building was empty by 10:15 p.m.

There wasn't any other movement on the surveillance system until just after 1:00 a.m. in the morning. One of the cameras picked up movement from an entry door just off the loading dock at the rear of the government center.

Chief Betts and Garcia both took a closer look at the monitor. A man dressed in blue pants, a gray button-up shirt, and dark-colored baseball hat entered the maintenance garage bay area.

"Is that door controlled by an electronic keycard?" Blake said, looking intently at the monitor.

"I don't think so. A few doors around the building still use a regular key. If I remember correctly, that is one of them," the chief said, adding, "Every door that uses an electronic keycard records the date, time, and whose keycard was used to open the door."

The chief pressed the pause button on the surveillance video and minimized the video screen. He logged onto a separate system and scrolled through the electronic keycard system.

"No, that door is still controlled by a normal key."

"What are the chances of that?" Garcia said aloud.

The chief opened up the surveillance system and pressed play on the video system.

From the present camera angle, it was hard to tell who the employee was. The man walked to the back of the bay area and opened a door that led into the basement hallway of the government center. The next set of cameras came to life as they sensed the movement. The man had a large, black backpack strapped to his back and he was carrying a large duffle bag. The button-up shirt he was wearing matched the government center's maintenance employees, and a white name tag was above the left breast pocket. All of the cameras so far were positioned near the ceiling and didn't provide a view of the subject's face. The guy definitely knew where he was going because there weren't any labels on the doors and he was taking a path that led straight to a back staircase.

Terror from Within

Once the man reached the staircase, he took the stairs two at a time and was soon on the main floor of the government center. He entered another hallway and proceeded directly to the restroom, which the first suspects had visited prior to the attack. Several minutes later, the man exited the restroom and continued past the circuit clerk's office. He reached the main staircase, which went to the second floor. The man looked around and then continued up the flight of stairs.

He reached the second floor and entered the men's restroom that was directly across the hallway from the staircase. A minute later, he exited the restroom empty handed and quickly walked back down the flight of stairs to the first floor.

The man retraced his path and returned to the basement of the government center. During the entire episode, it was impossible for them to get a view of the man's face. The cameras were positioned too high on the wall or the ceiling to be of any use.

"Are any of those other doors the guy used controlled by the electronic keycard system?"

The chief scrolled through a list. "No, he never entered an area that is controlled by that system"

"That guy doesn't look like any of the maintenance workers who left the building earlier in the evening," Garcia added. "The maintenance workers are always coming through our office to collect garbage and vacuum. I don't recognize him as someone who works here during the day. Is there a chance this guy was fired recently?"

The chief paused the video just as the man exited the building where he had initially entered. "We do all the hiring for the maintenance positions and we haven't fired anyone lately. We did have to lay off three people about a year ago. Let me pull up their photographs to see if someone matches that description."

He rolled his chair over to another computer that was set up away from the rows of monitors. The chief clicked on a few icons and pictures of the three former maintenance workers were displayed on the screen. "Considering we released two females and one male maintenance worker, it doesn't take a rocket scientist to see who our possible suspect is."

Garcia got up from his chair and walked over to the chief. He glanced over his shoulder and looked at the screen. "The guy in the video does resemble the man who was laid off. What was his name?"

"His name is Robert Whitlock."

Chapter 17

Correctional Officer Joanne Sullivan was called into the lieutenant's office prior to the afternoon roll call. She entered the office and shut the door behind her. One look at the lieutenant's face and she knew there was a problem.

She wasn't one to suck up to her commanders. She had worked in the jail for just over two years. She was always respectful of her commanders and rarely had a bad thing to say about them. With this being said, she didn't regularly visit the sergeant or lieutenant's office to shoot the breeze. After roll call was over, she would begin working at her assigned location even though a select few other correctional officers would stop by the sergeant's office and waste a half hour talking about things unrelated to work.

She sat down in a cloth-cushioned chair across the desk from the lieutenant and looked up at him. "You needed to see me, sir?"

The lieutenant got straight to the point. "Joanne, I need you to come with me upstairs. There has been a complaint brought against you, and we need to get your side of the story."

"What kind of complaint?"

The lieutenant stood up from his chair and said, "I'll have one of the detectives explain everything to you when we get to their office."

"Detectives?" Joanne said as she sat back down in the chair, a puzzled look on her face. "You know I've had complaints filed against me in the past, but it's never led to an interrogation."

The lieutenant tilted his head and glanced over his glasses. "Joanne, we really need your cooperation on this matter."

"If this is something you're accusing me of, then I'm not talking to anyone until I can speak with my lawyer."

"Joanne, nobody is accusing you of doing anything. Let's just see what the detective has to say, and then you can make your decision at that time. We're not going to force you to answer any questions. Let's go before roll call ends and everyone sees you leaving with me."

Joanne didn't like the idea of being blindsided by accusations. She knew the lieutenant was right about getting up to the investigations division before the other officers saw her leaving with the lieutenant. The rumors would fly rampant, and she would have no way of controlling them. "I'll see what he has to say, but I want it to be known that I want my lawyer present."

With that, they left the lieutenant's office and walked out of the administration bureau. They climbed a back staircase up to the investigations division. They were both quiet as the lieutenant rang the doorbell outside of the criminal investigations division.

Joanne's heart was racing, and the word criminal never seemed to be as in focus as it was today. She had assumed this day would come at some point, but even that didn't prepare her for what was possibly about to happen.

She snapped out of her trance as the door opened; a tall, somewhat good-looking detective held the door open.

Since the correctional facility employed such a large number of people, it was impossible for Blake to know all of them and he definitely hadn't seen Joanne prior to opening the door. She stood about five feet, four inches tall and had a medium build. Her hazel eyes were accented by her shoulder-length brown hair, which was pulled back into a ponytail. Her skin was tanned, and Blake noticed a wedding band on her left ring finger. This ring could potentially pose a barrier during the interview, Blake thought as he held the door open for them.

Blake had time prior to Joanne's arrival to complete a quick background check on her status at the sheriff's office. Prior to beginning her career with the sheriff's office, she held a dead-end secretarial position with a local travel agency. She began her career as a correctional officer with the sheriff's office in 2005. She attended a ten-week basic correctional officer academy, where she finished in the top of the class, academically. Her personnel file was off limits, so Blake had to go on what the chief knew about her. According to the chief, her name hadn't come up during any previous internal investigations.

Blake led them down the hallway and had Joanne sit in an interview room. He closed the door to the room and entered the AV room. He pushed the record button on the DVD player. Chief Kowalski and the lieutenant stayed in the AV room, and Blake and Sergeant McGuire entered the interview room with Joanne.

Blake shut the door behind them and took a seat next to Joanne. Sergeant McGuire remained standing and began. "Joanne, my name is Sergeant McGuire and this is Detective Talbot. We have a few things to go over with you and we'll explain why you're here."

"That would be great because I don't have the slightest clue why you guys pulled me up here."

"I'm sure you heard about the attack on the government center that occurred earlier this morning?" Sergeant McGuire began.

"I was called in early because of the incident but I know very little."

"Basically, we had several armed men attack a courtroom in the government center and escape with one of our inmates." The sergeant paused as he studied Joanne's reaction to the news. When she didn't even blink, he continued. "We've been working on this case since early this morning, and quite a few leads have developed in the investigation."

Joanne didn't wait for the sergeant to say another word before she interjected. "What does this have to do with me?"

"If you let me finish, I will explain this to you, unless you already know why we're talking to you, Ms. Sullivan," Sergeant McGuire said in a smart-ass tone.

Joanne winced at the little jab McGuire had just taken at her. Sergeant McGuire wasn't about to let her run the interview and it was obvious he was making it very clear from the start that he was the one asking questions.

"Now, as I was saying, we've been able to follow up on quite a few leads in the beginning stages of this investigation. One of those leads happens to come from a search we conducted of the escaped inmate's jail cell. If you know where I'm going with this conversation, please don't hesitate to jump in to let me know what's going on," he said to further drill home the point that he was running the interview. "A thorough search of this inmate's jail cell turned up a hollowed-out hole in one of the bed frames." Sergeant McGuire paused again to study Joanne's reaction. Her hands were still sitting on the table, and she hadn't blinked since he began speaking. "Inside that bed frame we located this cell phone." Sergeant McGuire slid a photocopy of the cell phone across the table to Joanne.

She took one look at it, and her face turned a slight shade of red. Blake could practically see her heart beating through her shirt. Joanne raised her left hand and nervously scratched the left side of her face.

"How would I know who hid that phone in the bed frame?" she said in a weak voice.

Blake leaned forward in his chair. "We're not saying you know who put the phone in the bed frame. We have information that you know how this cell phone was brought into the jail."

"People are able to smuggle things into the jail all the time. All they have to do is stick it in one of their body cavities, and it'll never be found. It's not like we do cavity searches on everyone who enters the jail."

"We're well aware of how someone is processed and booked into the jail," Sergeant McGuire exclaimed with an annoyed look on his face. "It would be one thing for someone to be processed and brought into the jail with contraband because they were hiding it from the police officer who arrested them. I've seen it happen many times where a criminal is hiding drugs in one of his or her body cavities." He paused again and scratched his forehead. "I've never seen someone hide a cell phone in a body cavity so that, when arrested, he'd have a way to communicate with someone outside of the jail."

"How stupid does she think we are?" Blake thought as he kept his eyes on Joanne. "Listen, this cell phone was smuggled into the jail, and we have reason to believe that you were the one who actually brought the phone into the jail. If this is a case where you were taken advantage of by an inmate who has enough time on his hands to manipulate a correctional officer, then we need to know the truth. If you continue to deny that you ever had any knowledge of the cell phone, then you're going to face felony conspiracy charges for facilitating the escape of an inmate. You will also be charged with official misconduct, which is a felony. Your days as a correctional officer would be over. Are you married, Ms. Sullivan?"

"Yeah."

"Any children?"

"Two."

"Do you want everyone to think that you are guilty of aiding in the escape of an inmate and the subsequent killing of a police officer? Is that how you want your family and friends to think of you? As a heartless traitor of the oath you had sworn to uphold?"

"No," was the only response she could muster, her head falling slowly into her hands.

"Joanne, I know you were trying to do the right thing when you provided the inmate with a cell phone," Blake added.

"I never planned for this to happen," she said as tears slowly cascaded down her cheeks. "I swear, I didn't know that he was planning to escape from the courthouse. He told me he just needed a way to contact his wife and children because his family didn't have enough money to pay the outrageous costs of purchasing phone cards through the jail's commissary."

Blake leaned a little closer towards Joanne as she continued welling up inside. He knew she was on the edge of filling them in on the entire story. He gently touched her right forearm, which was still sitting on the table. "Joanne, I know this is going to be tough for you, but we really need you to tell us the entire truth. You have to think about the family of the deceased police officer. If it were your family member who was killed, you would want things resolved as quickly as possible. If these guys are capable of killing one law enforcement officer, there is no telling where their trail of bloodshed will end."

Blake was familiar with the manipulation tactics used by the inmates. They had all day to sit around and think of ways to exploit the system. A good majority of them spent countless hours trying to groom a potential correctional officer into somewhat of an assistant for them. He had read studies on the simple everyday conversations between an inmate and a correctional officer and how the process began. The inmate would usually watch the officers and get to know some of their personal history. From there, they could select the most vulnerable officers and try to get some sort of dirt on them. It wasn't that the correctional officers were out trying to look for trouble. They happened to get caught up in the manipulation and usually didn't even see it happening until they were in over their heads.

After the first few minutes of this interview, Blake knew there was a good possibility that Joanne had fallen prey to the vicious tenacity of the inmates. Her uniform wasn't neatly pressed, even though she had just arrived at work. She appeared to be outwardly shy, a perfect target for an inmate who could praise her and show her signs that he was there to be her friend.

As Blake's thoughts continued to wander, Joanne continued. "That guy set me up for this big fall. He started out by acting as if he was my best friend. One day, I was assigned to work inside one of the cellblocks with the inmates. A second correctional officer was also assigned to keep an eye on the room with me. When that second officer went to a separate part of the block to follow up on an inquiry from an inmate, several of the other inmates confronted me. They were yelling and screaming and about to beat my brains in because I was a correctional officer. Just when I thought things were going to get real ugly, one of the inmates stepped in. He was able to control the group and divert a major ass whooping from occurring. From that day forward, I felt I owed him something." She paused and wiped her eyes again.

Blake slid a box of tissue across the table so she could wipe her tears. Joanne pulled out a tissue and blew her nose. She then dabbed the tears that were still streaming down her face.

"He came up to me several days after that incident and asked if I could get him a cigarette. At first, I told him I could get in big trouble for sneaking anything into the building for him. He told me that he thought he knew me better than that and proceeded to remind me that I had almost been jumped by an angry mob. I felt bad that he had stood up for me in front of a bunch of other inmates. That must have taken a lot of balls for him to do that." She shook her head as she thought about that inmate going out on a limb to help her. "I thought about it for a day, and then I came back to work with a pack of Newport 100s. I brought the pack into the jail along with several matches. During a casual conversation with the inmate, I was able to sneak him the pack of cigarettes and the matches."

"Did anyone ever get caught with the cigarettes?" Sergeant McGuire asked.

"Not to my knowledge. I made him promise to only smoke them when I was working in his cellblock. That way, nobody else would question the possibility of someone smoking in the cells. He was very thankful that I was able to help him. About a week later, he approached me and asked if I still wanted to be afforded some sort of protection when it came to my safety while inside the cellblocks. Of course, I wasn't about to continue sneaking him more cigarettes because I knew it just wasn't right. He asked if there was any way I could get him a few extra candy bars when the commissary came around. I figured an extra candy bar or two wasn't going to cause any harm, and he didn't have money to enjoy a candy bar. He said he also needed a pencil and a pad of paper, so he could write a letter to his family. This struck a soft spot in my heart because I could relate to not seeing family. I knew I would go crazy if I couldn't keep in contact with my family for some reason. So, I was able to sneak him a pencil and an extra pad of paper."

Sergeant McGuire was still standing and he couldn't believe what he was hearing. The details of what had become a major security breach were just spewing out of her mouth. It took all his restraint not to reach across the table and punch her in the face. If she wasn't so stupid and naïve, this escape probably wouldn't have ever happened. He continued to stare straight into her eyes. He was watching for any signs that she might be hiding more details than she was sharing. She seemed to be telling the truth during their interview. Sergeant McGuire knew that the inmate didn't have any immediate family members that he would be writing a letter to. The inmate had used these little favors as a way to slowly undermine her integrity and gain her trust. Sergeant McGuire knew all too well how this story was going to end.

Blake already knew the answer to the next question but he had to ask it anyway. "Did any other threats come your way during your time in their cellblock?"

"No, that was the good thing about this whole situation. I felt more control over the cellblock then I ever had before. My sergeant even complimented me on the way our block had shown a decrease in fights and lockdown incidents. It didn't take long for the other correctional officers to notice that I was doing such a good job. They all were wondering how a shy, reserved girl like me could run such a well-behaved group of criminals. I never let anyone onto the fact that it was as easy as providing one inmate with several small tokens of appreciation for the entire cellblock to straighten up. This went on for another week or so before the inmate decided he needed a more efficient way of communicating with his family. He told me a sad story about how his mom was battling cancer and she wasn't able to come to the jail to see him. He said he wasn't sure if she would live long enough to receive the letters he had mailed her."

Joanne's crying had subsided temporarily and her eyes darted back and forth between Blake and McGuire. "You guys wouldn't understand this part because you've never worked in the jail to see firsthand how devastating this can be for these inmates. Most of them grew up in underprivileged homes without any chance to lead a productive life in society. They come from single parent homes, where their next meal wasn't always a guarantee. To see this inmate have so much compassion towards his mother, it brought tears to my eyes."

Blake could tell she was really struggling with the fact that she had just aided in the escape of an inmate. She thought all along that she was doing something good for this inmate. These kinds of people weren't meant to be correctional officers, he thought. In her personal quest to help this inmate and society, she had broken every general order and law that would prohibit these sorts of actions. If she felt the need to help the less fortunate, she should have signed up to work at a local homeless shelter, Blake thought. Her actions would no doubt cause serious changes to the way the correctional officers interact with the inmate population.

Joanne continued with her side of the story. "One day, he came to me with a demand rather than a simple request. His idea of a more efficient way of speaking with his mother was to have me bring him a cell phone. He told me it needed to include text messaging capabilities. I told him that he had crossed the line, and this wasn't going to happen. He immediately became infuriated and threatened to kill me and my family. He told me the names of my family members and even my home address. He threatened to expose the previous favors I had provided him. I didn't want my family to be harmed, so I finally agreed to help him out one last time. He told me to purchase a pre-paid cell phone at a local store. He said that I needed to pay with cash, and he even slid me five hundred dollars cash to help pay for the phone. I never asked him where he got the cash from. He told me I could keep the change after I paid for the phone."

She suddenly began shaking as the gravity of her actions were slowing catching up with her. Blake reached over and patted her on the back, trying to console her.

"You're doing a great job, Joanne."

The shaking continued as she kept talking. "The next morning, before work, I went and purchased a pre-paid cell phone. I paid for unlimited calls and text messages for the first three months. When I arrived at work, I was assigned to transport this inmate to one of his court dates. On the way down to the courtroom, I was able to give him the cell phone. I told him this was the last favor I could do for him."

"Did he ever tell you he needed to speak with anyone besides his mother?" Sergeant McGuire asked.

"No, he seemed very concerned about his mother."

"You seem to have gotten to know him fairly well. If you had to guess, where do you think he would go after he escaped?" Sergeant McGuire continued.

"I really think he would travel to see his mother before he went anywhere else."

"Is there anything else you can think of that could assist us in our investigation?" Blake added as he slid his chair away from the table. "Even if it's something small, it could go a long way in assisting us with tracking him down."

"I can't think of anything right now."

"Okay, give Sergeant McGuire and I a few minutes, and we'll be right back with you."

They left the interview room and closed the door behind them. They walked down the short hallway and entered the conference room. Chief Kowalski and the lieutenant exited the AV room and walked into the conference room.

"We're going to place Joanne on administrative leave effective immediately. This will allow you guys time to complete your investigation," Chief Kowalski said, his face flushed red.

"Right now, we're going to hold off on seeking formal charges against her. Our main concern is tracking down these suspects. We can always meet with the SA down the road to file criminal charges against her," Sergeant McGuire said.

They went over several highlights of the interview and made sure they had covered all the aspects of the investigation. They decided to have her relinquish all of her county property, including her uniform, badge, and electronic keycard.

Sergeant McGuire and Blake followed the lieutenant down the hallway and into the interview room.

"Effective immediately, you are being placed on administrative leave. I'll bring you back downstairs, and a female commander will escort you into the women's locker room to change back into your civilian clothes. She'll collect all of your county-issued property, and you'll be free to leave," the lieutenant calmly told Joanne.

"You've got to be kidding me!" Joanne yelled as she slammed her fist onto the table. "How can you guys do this to me? I've got children to feed and bills to pay."

"Joanne, I understand you're frustrated, but we've got a job to do and unfortunately, sometimes your actions may have consequences you don't agree with," the lieutenant added.

"I've never done anything like this before. I can't believe that I don't get a second chance," Joanne said, tears pouring down her face.

With that, Joanne stood up and the lieutenant escorted her out of the interview room. Blake led them to the front door of detective bureau and watched as they disappeared down the hallway.

Chapter 18

The court security officer located the sheriff amongst the rubble on the first floor of the government center and passed along the message from Chief Betts. The sheriff was covered from head to toe in gray dust from the falling debris.

Recue crews from several local fire departments were on scene trying to locate anyone who might be trapped in the rubble. The command center was in charge of coordinating the entire investigation, and one patrol sergeant was assigned to keep track of where every investigator was at any given time. Initial reports said that five investigators were unaccounted for after the blast.

The sheriff picked up a telephone that was situated near the north entrance and dialed the extension for the surveillance center.

"Chief, can you make arrangements for us to move the command center and the staging areas to the secure room in the basement?"

The government center housed a large, safe room in the basement that could be used to run a major disaster. There were computers, televisions, and fax machines all set up for this sort of incident.

"I'll have one of my guys run downstairs to make sure all the doors are unlocked," Chief Betts added.

"Thank you. I'll let the guys at the command post know that they can move to the secure room." With that, the sheriff hung up the telephone.

The sheriff walked over to the command post and advised them to pick up their belongings and move to the secure room in the basement. There weren't any complaints from the guys who were tasked with coordinating the entire multi-agency investigation. Within a few minutes, they had all vacated the atrium and had relocated to the secure room in the basement.

The sheriff returned to the telephone in the atrium and contacted the county 911 dispatch center to ask them to contact the ATF. He wanted to make sure that the ATF was responding to the government center to assist with the investigation into the explosion. He also asked the dispatcher to send over the first available bomb-sniffing dog so the entire government center could be safely cleared before any further investigation in the building resumed. The sheriff wasn't going to risk the possibility of another explosive device sitting in the government center waiting to kill more first responders.

☙❧

Blake attended a 6:00 p.m. intelligence meeting in the safe room in the government center. A representative from each crime scene location presented an update of the investigation. Ideas were brought up on what the next phase of the investigation should include. Sheriff Calhoun thanked everyone for his or her support and assistance during this major incident. It was decided that the investigators would work day and night until an arrest was made in the case. Several investigators commented on what it would be like if they were the ones who had died, and the investigators went home before following up on any open leads.

The SWAT team had previously departed the rest stop and was on standby back at the government center prior to the intelligence meeting. After the meeting, the team was split into several groups and assigned to check several prior addresses for the escaped prisoner.

Garcia and Blake were assigned to track down Robert Whitlock's soon-to-be ex-wife. Garcia had completed a preliminary background investigation on Robert and his wife before attending the intelligence briefing. They located court documents showing that Robert's wife Sara had filed for an order of protection and, at the same time, filed paperwork for dissolution of marriage. Robert was kicked out of the house after he was served his copy of the OP, and he wasn't supposed to have contact with anyone at the residence, including his children.

Garcia and Blake left the government center and jumped into Blake's county car. They exited the parking lot and drove east towards Belcher.

During their drive across town, they analyzed the current state of the investigation. There was no information obtained that would allow for any connection between Robert and any sort of organized crime. Robert's rise from a relatively obscure existence in the eyes of law enforcement to a major role in the biggest attack on a government body in the entire state of Michigan was mind-boggling. The million-dollar question became who was Robert working for and where were they headed?

They arrived at Sara's street and drove around the block several times to make sure there weren't any suspicious vehicles in the area. The last thing they needed was to be ambushed while approaching the house.

It was still light outside as Blake parked his car several houses down from where Sara lived. Without the cover of darkness, they would be seen well before they could approach the house.

Several SWAT team members were assigned to assist Blake and Garcia, and they parked their cars near Blake's. The two SWAT officers went around to the rear of the residence and secured themselves behind a dense tree line. They kept their eyes on the residence for any signs of trouble.

Blake, Garcia, and the rest of the group approached the front door. They were wearing their pullover ballistic vests, which had the word "SHERIFF" written in bold letters across the front and rear. From the front window, Blake could see a female watching television with her back to him. He scanned the room, and there were no signs of anyone else present in the house.

As Blake kept an eye on the female who was sitting on the couch, Garcia pressed the doorbell. A chime echoed within the house. The female instinctively turned around to see who was at the door. She got up from the couch and her eyes widened as she saw who was ringing the doorbell. She unlocked the deadbolt and pulled the steel entry door wide open.

"Ma'am, we're with the sheriff's department and we need to speak with you for a second," Garcia said.

"Sure, what's going on?"

"Is Robert home?"

"No, he's not allowed at the house because of the OP I have against him."

"Would you allow us to double check to make sure he didn't sneak in without your knowledge?"

"He's not here. Can I ask what this is in regards to?"

"Well, we have reason to believe that he's somehow involved with today's incident at the government building in Three Forks. We just want to make sure you and your children aren't in any danger."

"We're fine. That incident has been all over the news, and I don't think Robert would have anything to do with something like that. He does have a drinking problem, but he would never do anything of that magnitude."

She opened the door and motioned for them to enter the house.

"If we could just check out the house real quick to make sure he's not here, then we can get more information from you," Garcia added, his eyes scanning the room.

"Go ahead. The children are in their rooms doing their homework. I'll run up there to let them know that you are here."

They tactically searched the entire house from top to bottom and didn't locate any signs of Robert. Most of Robert's belongings were packed into boxes in the basement and were waiting to be picked up. Blake and Garcia returned to the living room to speak with Sara.

"Do you have Robert's cell phone number?" Blake asked.

Sara grabbed her phone off the end table. "I don't know his number off the top of my head," she said, scrolling through her contact list. She located the number and provided it to them. "Can you tell me how he may be involved in this?"

"Right now we can't disclose any information about the investigation other than what was released during the press conference earlier today. I wish we could tell you everything will be fine, but we're not exactly sure what he's been up to. Do you know who he has been hanging out with since he was served with the OP?"

"Not really. I have heard through some mutual friends that he's been hanging out at the Legend in Belcher."

Blake knew from previous intelligence reports that the Legend had a fairly large-scale drug operation being run through the business. The area narcotics enforcement group wasn't able to get a case on the owner because he had several underlings pushing the drugs for him. If Blake read a recent narcotics intelligence bulletin correctly, it was alleged that a kilo of cocaine was being pushed out the doors every month.

"So, you haven't heard any names floating around about who he's been running with?"

"I did hear someone say they saw Robert having a beer with his old buddy, John Gibson. Robert knows him from our son's little league baseball team. I don't know where John lives now."

"Can you think of anything else that may assist us in finding Robert?"

"I don't think so. He drives his black pickup truck everywhere, so if you find his truck, you'll most likely find him."

"We really appreciate you being cooperative with us."

Blake pulled a business card out of his wallet and wrote his cell phone number on the back of it.

"If Robert happens to call you or stop by after we leave, please call my cell phone ASAP." He handed her the business card and thanked her for her time.

Blake and Garcia exited the residence and walked back towards their car. After contacting the other officers via their portable radios to let them know they were free to leave the area, they jumped back into their unmarked squad car.

"Do you believe her?" Garcia added as Blake pulled the gear shifter into drive.

"I think she's telling us the truth. The OP's been valid for a while and she would have no reason to be lying about Robert's whereabouts."

"I ran their names through our database, and it doesn't show any incidents between them since the OP was filed."

It seemed odd to Blake that he actually believe her comments; over the years, he had become skeptical because the majority of people would lie directly to his face without showing any signs of being deceitful.

He remembered one of his first few months as a patrol deputy. He was attempting to serve a warrant at a residence. He did his background on the wanted person and everything indicated that he lived at one particular address. He had conducted pre-surveillance and hadn't noticed any action at the house, and when he knocked on the door, a boy who appeared to be about eight years old answered. Blake had asked to speak with the wanted person and the boy said he wasn't sure if that person was home. The boy went downstairs into the basement and returned two minutes later and said that the wanted person wasn't home. Sensing that something wasn't right because of the circumstances, he grilled the boy about when he last saw the wanted person. After about ten minutes of questioning, the little boy finally folded and told him that the wanted person was, in fact, downstairs in a bedroom. He remembered subsequently taking the wanted person into custody and wondering why an eight year old would lie to the police.

It was his ability to sort through all of the lies and bullshit that allowed Blake to become a better police officer. So, it wasn't out of the ordinary for Garcia to be questioning what Sara had relayed to them. They just had to go with their gut instincts for the time being and believe her until they could prove otherwise.

Garcia turned the in-car laptop computer towards him and double clicked on the Internet icon. After logging into their main intelligence database, he typed Robert's cell phone number into the search field and then hit the submit button. The computer screen refreshed, and the cell phone carrier was listed. Garcia was able to locate an exigent circumstances form for Robert's cell phone carrier and he filled in all the blanks. There was enough circumstantial evidence to conclude that Robert was somehow involved in the incident at the government center. He included a brief synopsis of the day's events and included why Robert was a suspect. He then sent an e-mail to the cell phone carrier requesting they provide him with all recent activity, including any cell towers the phone may be pinging off. The last time Garcia had to deal with a cell phone carrier, they were able to respond within ten minutes as to the cell phone's current location. He hoped that today wasn't going to be any different.

Blake pulled his car into the parking lot of a local fire station, and Garcia picked up his cell phone to call Sergeant McGuire.

"Hey, Sarge, it's Garcia. Can you have someone drive by the Legend in Belcher? We need to see if Robert's black pickup truck is in the area. If you're able to find it, can you have a team set up surveillance on it? We're trying to see if his cell phone is on and if it's hitting off any cell phone towers in the area."

"Sure, I'll head that way right now. I'll call you in a little bit to keep you updated."

"Thanks."

Garcia hung up the phone and placed it back into his pocket. "Robert is going to be the key to locating where these guys are hiding out. If he is the one who planted the guns inside of the government center, then we need to get him now."

"I know the county maintenance guys have a pre-employment background check done, but how did Robert slip through the cracks?"

"What do you mean?" Garcia said as he looked over at Blake.

"Well, I've been looking up previous cases involving Robert's family. The reports indicate that Robert had a rough life while growing up. Robert's father bounced around from dead-end job to dead-end job. According to the reports from the police and the Department of Child and Family Services, his father was an alcoholic and cokehead who spent long stretches of Robert's young life bouncing in and out of prison. He seemed to always collect some sort of government handout and managed to squander it away on more booze and drugs."

The reports indicate his mother had dropped out of high school in the tenth grade when she had become pregnant with Robert's older brother. Her frequent drug use kept her from ever getting a real boyfriend as she bounced around from junkie to junkie. Robert was born when his mother was only nineteen years old. She rented a bedroom at a local motel; it didn't even have a kitchen or refrigerator in the room. She married Robert's father when she was twenty-one, and they continued living in a small motel room in downtown Lansing."

"It's not that someone can't turn their life around, but it doesn't look like Robert ever had a chance," Blake said as he continued scanning through the reports. "Robert grew up with his father constantly abusing his mother. They were both heavy drug users, and it's nearly impossible for someone to break that vicious cycle once they've been dragged into it."

"But, he had a stable job working for the county prior to being laid off. Why would he suddenly get caught up in this mess?"

Garcia's cell phone rang and interrupted their conversation.

"Hello?"

"Hey, I had one of our undercover narcotics guys drive through the parking lot, and Robert's truck is there. They've got eyes on the truck, and I can let you know if it moves at all," Sergeant McGuire said.

Terror from Within

"We haven't received the information back from the cell phone carrier. As soon as it comes back, I'll give you a call. If anything changes, please call me right away."

"I will."

Garcia hung up the phone and turned to Blake. "They've located Robert's truck at the Legend. I'll refresh my e-mail account to see if the cell phone company returned the exigent circumstances form."

The computer screen refreshed, and he had a new message in his inbox. He opened the e-mail and quickly read through it. The e-mail had an attachment that had all of the pertinent cell phone information listed in chronological order.

Garcia turned the computer screen so it was facing towards Blake.

"Look at this," Garcia said. "His cell phone is being triangulated to these GPS coordinates."

Garcia opened a second Internet browser and typed the GPS coordinates into the appropriate boxes in the mapping system. He zoomed into the map to get a better view of where the cell phone was located. The coordinates showed the cell phone was in Riverside County, which was two hours northwest of Humble County.

"There goes our possibility of him being at the Legend," Blake added.

"We still need to make an appearance inside of the Legend to make sure Robert's not in there."

"We'll need to contact the Riverside County Sheriff's Department to see if they are familiar with that location."

"Hopefully, this will be the break we've been looking for."

Blake placed a cell phone call to Detective Sergeant McGuire and filled him in on the location of Robert's cell phone.

Sergeant McGuire filled Blake in on the plan to have several of the undercover narcotics detectives check inside of the Legend to make sure that Robert wasn't in there.

Blake pressed the end button on this phone and connected it to his car charger. He hadn't charged his battery the night before because of his vacation plans. He always left his cell phone home during his vacations, so he could completely forget about the stresses of the job.

Meanwhile, Garcia had located a link on the Internet for the Riverside County Sheriff's Department. He clicked on the link and contact information for the sheriff's department showed up on the screen. He pulled out his cell phone and called the telephone number listed on the screen.

"Hello, could I please speak with one of your detectives?" Garcia said into the phone.

A dispatcher on the other end advised him that their only detective wasn't in the office.

"My name is Detective Garcia from the Humble County Sheriff's Department. Is there any way I could speak with a patrol supervisor?"

The dispatcher told him that the supervisor was out on the road, and she would have to take his cell number to have the supervisor call him back. Garcia provided the dispatcher with his cell phone number and then thanked her for the assistance.

Garcia's cell phone rang several minutes later. The male on the other end introduced himself as a patrol sergeant for the Riverside County Sheriff's Department. Garcia provided him with some pertinent information regarding their current investigation. He asked the sergeant if they had any calls for service to the area where the cell phone was triangulating to. The sergeant didn't seem too surprised when Garcia described the area to him. The supervisor went on to explain how the land was owned by an anti-government group that often trained its members on the sprawling, secluded, one-hundred-acre compound.

Chapter 19
Belcher, MI

Detective Sergeant McGuire held an impromptu intelligence briefing in the parking lot behind a local school. Four undercover detectives and a confidential informant were assigned to scope out the Legend for any signs of Robert or John.

Sergeant McGuire passed out photographs of both individuals so the detectives could familiarize themselves with who they were looking for. The CI drew up a floor plan of the Legend and distributed it to the detectives. They reviewed the floor plan to make sure there weren't any logistical issues with the operations plan. The UCs were all wired with tiny hidden surveillance cameras and wireless listening devices. The plan called for Sergeant McGuire and several of the SWAT team members to be waiting outside in a surveillance vehicle to monitor the situation via the AV feeds from inside the bar. After the detectives were done setting up the various cameras and audio devices, they ran a test to make sure everything was functioning properly, and after everything appeared to be working properly, the UCs and the CI departed the parking lot.

Sergeant McGuire and five SWAT members all entered a green, full-size surveillance van. Sergeant McGuire retrieved a magnetic sign from inside of the van and placed it on the side of the van. The sign indicated that the van was owned by a local construction company. One of the SWAT team members drove the van and the rest of the guys sat in the rear. This surveillance vehicle was purchased using a federal Department of Homeland Security grant. The back windows of the van were completely blacked out. A shelving unit was mounted directly behind the front seats, which fit the part of the construction business at the same time providing the occupants in the rear with complete cover. A small shelf held two monitors that allowed them to record and watch live video feeds from the tiny cameras secured on the UCs. Connected to each monitor was an audio jack set up to record and listen live to the UCs' conversations. A few pairs of headphones were in a clear bin next to the monitors. Four lightweight chairs were bolted to the floor to minimize movement in the van while it was parked and in surveillance mode. A separate AV surveillance system, including a boom microphone, was mounted into the ladder rack on the top of the van. This system allowed the occupants to observe and hear what was going on outside of the van without having to look out the windows or open the doors. A small dehumidifier was mounted below the monitors, allowing the detectives to sit inside of the van for extended periods of time without having the windows fog up. A small portable toilet was bolted to the floor in the rear of the van, surrounded by a curtain.

They drove the van to the parking lot of the Legend and parked just as the clock on the dashboard turned to 9:17 p.m. The plainclothes deputy got out and walked away from the van. He disappeared around the back of the

Legend and followed a footpath that led to an apartment complex behind the bar. Another detective driving an unmarked car picked up the deputy in the parking lot of the apartment complex.

Sergeant McGuire started up the computer monitors and logged onto the live AV feeds that were coming from the UCs. He could see that they were driving in two separate vehicles towards the bar. They all watched the monitors as the UCs pulled into the parking lot of the Legend. They parked their vehicles and entered the bar.

As soon as they entered the bar, the monitors from the live feeds of the UCs went blank.

"What the hell is wrong with this thing?" Sergeant McGuire said as he quickly shut down the program and restarted the system. Once it rebooted, Sergeant McGuire logged back on, and a small message showed up on the screen. The message said that there weren't any live feeds available. "You've got to be kidding me. What are the chances that this system goes down right now?"

That's when Sergeant McGuire remembered reading several officer safety intelligence bulletins within the past year. The bulletins warned of organized criminals using scrambling devices that could potentially disrupt police communication devices or cell phone signals.

Sergeant McGuire's mind was spinning. "We need to get in contact with our UCs. We're going to have to abort this operation if we can't monitor what's going on inside," he said to the rest of the SWAT members who were sitting in the van.

Sergeant McGuire opened up his cell phone and scrolled down until he reached Lieutenant Young's contact information. He pressed the send button and listened as the phone began ringing. Lieutenant Young answered the phone after the second ring, and Sergeant McGuire filled him in on the lack of contact with the UCs. Lieutenant Young advised Sergeant McGuire to pull the plug on the operation because the risks far outweighed the rewards for this operation. Sergeant McGuire pressed the end button on his phone. Then he dialed the number for one of the Ucs and the call went directly to voicemail. Sergeant McGuire tried the telephone numbers for the other UCs, and all of their phones went directly to voicemail, which usually indicated that the phone wasn't receiving a signal.

This operation was going to hell in a hand basket real fast, Sergeant McGuire thought, trying to come up with a way to contact the UCs who were inside of the bar. There weren't any additional UCs available to enter the Legend to pass the word along that the surveillance system wasn't working properly. He decided to go against Lieutenant Young's advice of potentially blowing the cover of the UCs and just keep an eye on the exterior of the bar.

The next hour dragged by as Sergeant McGuire and the rest of the team stared intently at the monitor, which showed a live video feed of the front door of the Legend. Several people had come and gone from the bar, but there was no sign of the UCs. They obviously hadn't tried to make any phone calls, Sergeant McGuire thought. Otherwise, they would have surely walked outside after realizing there was no service inside the bar.

Sergeant McGuire wasn't surprised that the criminals had the money and ability to block electronic devices from transmitting from inside of their business. It was comical that the county didn't even have the ability to block the transmission of electronic devices from inside of its own correctional facility. There had been some recent case law being analyzed by several state supreme courts that would determine if this sort of electronic jamming could be constitutionally allowed inside of correctional facilities. The capabilities of these systems had improved greatly over the past decade, and could now effectively be installed in a jail without disrupting the normal calls being made by correctional officers or attorneys. Sergeant McGuire had a hard time believing that a jail or prison couldn't implement a system that would eliminate the ability for criminals to illegally communicate to the outside world.

This created a massive security issue for witnesses and the general public. Sergeant McGuire thought about several recent news articles from across the country where the illegal use of cell phones from inside of correctional institutions was on the rise. Criminals were using the phones to run their drug enterprises and even kill witnesses. It was just a matter of time before the national news media caught wind of this loophole and something was done to correct it.

It was approaching 10:35 p.m. and the UCs had been in the Legend for over an hour without any means of communicating with their backup. The worst-case scenario kept playing out in Sergeant McGuire's mind. If the owner had the ability to electronically jam the wireless devices, there was a good chance he invested in an electronic eavesdropping detector. If the owner had caught on to the UCs, he could have used some of his bouncers to force them into a second-floor office. From there, all bets were off as to the UCs' safety, and even the safety of the undercover van could be in jeopardy.

Just then, the front door opened and two of the UCs walked out the front door with the CI. They got into their undercover vehicle and left the parking lot.

Sergeant McGuire's cell phone rang as he watched the UC vehicle exit the parking lot.

"What the hell is going on in there?" he whispered into the phone.

It wasn't that he didn't trust the UCs operating without any communication, it was the fact that they were potentially dealing with a major criminal organization that had just pulled off the most brazen attack one could ever imagine.

"Everything is fine, why?" one of the UCs asked.

"We weren't able to monitor any of your activities since you entered the bar. The owner must have some sort of jamming device installed inside of the building. Were you able to pick up any useful leads?"

"Robert and John weren't inside the bar," the UC said. "I'll fill you in with more information at the debriefing."

Sergeant McGuire was still watching the monitor and saw the last two UCs exit the bar. They walked across the parking lot and got into their car. The headlights turned on, and the car left the parking lot.

"Okay, the other two just left. We'll hang back for a bit, and then we can debrief back at the school parking lot."

Terror from Within

"Roger that; we'll be there waiting for you," the UC said.

The surveillance van left the parking lot just after 11:00 p.m. Within several minutes, they were all parked behind the school. They held a debriefing on what had occurred inside of the Legend and the fact that the UCs didn't overhear anyone talking about the attack on the government center.

"At this point, we're not sure if this bar has any association to the events that unfolded earlier today. If you guys could send out a notice to the other UCs to let them know about the troubles we had trying to electronically monitor the activities from inside of the bar, it would be greatly appreciated," Sergeant McGuire added as he jotted down several notes.

After the debriefing, everyone drove back to the government center to await another assignment. They arrived at the government center and were able to take a break inside of the sheriff's department's training division. The deputies used the time to catch a quick nap. News had filtered in about the location of Robert's cell phone.

Everyone was eager to get further details on the connection between the anti-government group and Humble County. Thus far, nothing in the investigation connected the dots between the escaped prisoner, Robert, and the anti-government group.

Blake and Garcia arrived back at the government center just after midnight. The fatigue was beginning to take its toll on everyone involved in the investigation. They had all been working diligently since the initial attack, which occurred over sixteen hours ago. They went to the training division to check in with the other investigators.

Blake grabbed a water out of the refrigerator and took a few sips as he sat down at one of the tables in the training room. His thoughts drifted towards his wife and kids at home. The entire family had been waiting for several months to finally be able to go on this vacation, and now it didn't look like it was going to work out. It was still tough to explain to his young children why their dad had to go to work at such inconvenient times. Blake made up his mind that he'd have to make this up to them once this investigation was completed.

Garcia opened up his Toughbook laptop computer. The sergeant from the Riverside Sheriff's Department was going to e-mail him several police reports dealing with their contacts at the location where Robert might be hiding out. He logged onto the e-mail system and opened up his inbox. There were several e-mails from the sergeant. He opened the first e-mail, which included a short summary of the people who were known to live at the residence. Attached to the e-mail were copies of several of the police reports. Blake printed off the police reports and then walked over to the printer to gather all of the reports.

As several deputies were catching a quick nap, Blake returned to the table and reviewed each police report.

The first report was taken in the spring of 1995 and was right after the group purchased the land. The sheriff's department had responded to an anonymous report of automatic gunfire coming from the property. The first deputies on scene were unable to make entry onto the property because of a large gate across the entrance to the

Terror from Within

driveway. A representative from the group had noticed the squad car parked at the entrance and spoke with the deputies. The report went on to state that the landowners denied the deputies permission to enter onto the property. Without any evidence of any illegal activity, the deputies were forced to leave the area empty handed.

There were many police reports generated between the initial report and now. As Blake continued reading through the reports, he could tell that the group was becoming more and more brazen as time went on.

One report in late 1999 raised suspicion that the group was holding training sessions for an anti-government militia. There were numerous reports of explosions coming from the property. When the deputies responded to the location, they were told to stay off the property, otherwise they would be shot. This of course didn't sit well with the sheriff or his deputies, but the sheriff believed the incident could be resolved peacefully so he ordered his deputies to stay off the property until a further notice.

Just about the same time that these explosions were reported, the group had stopped paying property taxes. Deputies were sent to the property several times in an attempt to serve the owners with civil court papers, and they were constantly turned away by the inability to make direct contact with anyone on the property.

At one point early in 2005, the sheriff's department sought assistance from several different federal agencies, including the FBI and the ATF.

A plan was established to shut off all power to the property and see what would transpire. The power was turned off to the property in September of 2006, and it didn't seem to bother the people who lived there. There was a small river running through the property and the house was reported to have several large wood-burning fireplaces.

The problem continued to be a thorn in the side of local law enforcement. The local news media ran several articles in the newspaper about the group's tactics. The sheriff was quoted as saying that he wasn't about to start a world war over this situation. He was interested in trying to peacefully resolve the situation no matter how long it took.

Throughout the years, the sheriff's department tried many different types of surveillance of the group. They were able to wire up a video surveillance device capable of monitoring one of the property's outbuildings. This system was left up for several weeks before it was dismantled because it didn't provide any useful information.

Garcia pulled a chair up next to Blake. "Did they e-mail you those reports?"

Blake slid some of the reports across the table. "Yeah, look at all of these. It doesn't look like this case is going to be wrapped up anytime soon if they are connected with this anti-government group."

Garcia read the reports, and his eyebrows rose slightly. He couldn't believe what he was reading. The group had taken control over its property and they were doing everything they could to function without government interaction.

"Can you believe that they have even threatened to shoot at the deputies if they come onto the property?" Blake added.

Terror from Within

"These reports are absolutely mind-boggling; it seems like the sheriff has recently decided to try and let the entire situation blow over. They stopped all surveillance operations and even ceased their efforts to respond to the property over any complaints, since things weren't spilling over into the community and affecting average citizens' lives. I sent the sergeant an e-mail and requested we set up an intelligence meeting with them to determine if these guys could, in fact, be involved in our incident."

Sheriff Calhoun and Sergeant McGuire entered the room as Blake finished reading the last report. He briefed them both on the situation in Riverside County. It was decided that they would try to meet with representatives from the Riverside County Sheriff's Department as soon as possible.

The sheriff updated everyone on the progress with the search and rescue in the rubble on the first floor of the government center.

"There are still two detectives who are unaccounted for," the sheriff said, trying to keep his voice steady. "The search and rescue teams are in place and have started to slowly sift through the rubble. A dog has been brought in to aid in the search efforts, and I'm confident that these detectives will be located. If everyone could please join me in a moment of silence, as we reflect on today's tragic events..."

The sheriff finished speaking and then sat down in a chair next to the podium. The entire room had fallen silent when the news broke about the two detectives.

The sheriff then made a decision to send the detectives home for the remainder of the night to catch up on sleep. He requested that they meet at 6:00 a.m. in the morning to continue working on the remaining leads in the case.

The deputies from the SWAT team were assigned to provide around-the-clock assistance to the court security officers with securing the government center. The SWAT team left the training division to meet up with several of the court security officers who were still securing the government center.

Blake left the government center at 1:07 a.m. and climbed into his unmarked squad car. His legs were throbbing with a dull ache, as he wasn't use to being on his feet for an entire day. Blake doubted that he would be able to fall asleep once he arrived home. He pulled his car out of the parking lot and continued down Grand River Avenue, passing the rows of television news crews that were still stationed down the street. He had to admire the dedication of the news reporters who were still mingling in the area long after the incident.

He arrived home and pulled into the garage. He exited his car and let the door shut behind him. He entered the mudroom and took off his jacket before hanging it on one of the hooks mounted to the wall. His wife's suitcase was still sitting in the laundry room, waiting to be loaded into the family minivan. There was a small light on in the kitchen, and it cast long shadows across the dining room and into the living room. He slipped off his shoes and quietly walked through the living room and up the stairs to the second floor. He checked on the children, and they were sound asleep. The door to his bedroom was ajar and creaked as he opened it. Maria was sleeping soundly on the bed. He brushed his teeth and then changed into a pair of pajamas. Blake slipped into bed, pulled the covers over himself, and was sound asleep as soon as his head hit the pillow.

Chapter 20
Wednesday, June 20th, Three Forks, MI

The alarm went off at 4:45 a.m. and Blake rolled over and turned it off. He got out of bed and took a warm shower. He had slept like a baby and actually felt somewhat rested as he stepped out of the shower. He dried himself off and wrapped the towel around his waist, and he couldn't help but notice the toll fast food restaurants were taking on his physique. He wasn't quite sure how he had allowed himself to become so out of shape. During his time in high school, he played on the varsity hockey and baseball teams. He was in peak physical shape during those years, and it didn't seem to matter what he ate. As the years went on, his time was mostly consumed with his family and work, which didn't leave any time to run to the gym a few times a week. He made a promise to himself to start some sort of workout regimen once this case wrapped up.

He finished shaving and then pulled on a pair of black dress pants, a blue button-up shirt, and completed the outfit with a matching tie. He grabbed the matching suit coat and draped it over his arm. He paused by the side of the bed and gently kissed Maria on the cheek. She hadn't even flinched as he was getting ready for work. There was little doubt that she was exhausted from working a full-time job and juggling the responsibilities of parenting.

Blake quietly left the bedroom and closed the door behind him. He ate a bowl of cereal and drank a cup of orange juice.

He wrote a short note to Maria explaining why he had to go back to work and that he'd call her later in the morning. He placed a few snacks into his lunchbox and walked out into the garage. The garage was cool, and there was a bright stream of sunlight starting to come through the windows on the garage door. Blake hit the button for the garage door and it rattled open. It was a subtle reminder to have the tracks greased to avoid any future problems.

Blake eased his car out of the driveway and shut the white garage door behind him. He waved to his neighbor, who was sitting on his porch, enjoying the summer morning. Blake thought he surely wouldn't mind being retired and having the ability to enjoy the mornings, but on the other hand, his children were still small and he hated to see them grow up too fast. The days already seemed to be flying by, and he just couldn't imagine them going any faster. It seemed like just yesterday that their first child was born, and now his oldest was going to attend kindergarten in the fall.

He worked his way through the light morning traffic and arrived at the government center at 5:49 a.m. Most of the news agencies were still staged down the street and their large antennas were hoisted high into the sky.

The area in front of the government center where the blast had damaged the windows and wall was completely enclosed in a large, white barrier. This secured the scene

Terror from Within

and kept the news media from watching every move of the investigators.

The county administrator had made the decision the previous night to close the government center for the remainder of the week so that every possible piece of evidence could be collected.

Already on the scene to handle the investigation into the explosion were guys in dark-blue windbreakers with the letters ATF written on the back.

Blake hadn't received any sort of training into explosions, and he couldn't think of anyone else in the county who would have the training necessary to conduct that sort of investigation. Also, with an investigation this big, it didn't hurt to have as much assistance as possible.

Blake parked in the back of the government center and used his electronic keycard to enter the building at the sheriff's entrance. He walked down the empty halls and into the training room. He logged onto his laptop computer and checked his e-mail.

The sergeant from Riverside County had responded to Blake's previous e-mail and had set up a meeting at 1:00 p.m. at his office. Blake responded to the e-mail and confirmed that he could meet with them at the specified time. Garcia agreed to travel with Blake to the meeting.

The morning briefing started promptly at 6:00 a.m. The sheriff started out by explaining that the search and rescue teams had completed sifting through the rubble from the explosion just after 4:00 a.m. this morning.

"This is one of the toughest things I've had to do in my entire career in law enforcement," the sheriff said as he started to wipe the tears that formed in the corners of his eyes. "Just after three o'clock this morning, two of our brothers were found deceased in the rubble. Detective Lange and Detective Riezinger from the Three Forks Police Department were two of the finest police officers to have ever worn the badge. As I stand here today, words can't describe the feeling I have for the utter disregard for human life that these suspects have shown towards our community. We won't rest until all of the individuals responsible for this devastation are brought to justice. I ask each and every one of you to please say a prayer for the families who have been devastated by the events of the past twenty-four hours. There will be grief counselors available as long as they are needed to assist everyone during these tough times. I know every one of you will be vigilant in your search for these cowardly criminals. Thank you for your dedication and please be safe out there," the sheriff said. "There are black bands on the table at the back of the room for everyone to place on their badges, in honor of our two fallen comrades."

A moment of silence was observed for the two detectives who were killed in the explosion.

Blake then caught everyone up to speed with his portion of the investigation, which led him to the property in Riverside County.

A commander from the ATF updated everyone on the status of their investigation. "We've had the chance to run a bomb-sniffing dog throughout the entire government center overnight, and no other explosive devices were located. The initial investigation has revealed that the suspects had rigged Pentaerythritol tetranitrate to a stall in the bathroom. When one of the detectives opened the stall door, it triggered the PETN to explode," the ATF commander said.

Sergeant McGuire ordered around-the-clock surveillance on Robert's truck until he could be located.

One of the groups left the government center to provide physical surveillance John Gibson's residence located on the south side of Belcher.

Several of the other detectives left the briefing to canvass the entire government center and look for any evidence. They began examining the bathrooms the suspects had entered prior to the attack.

Blake returned to his office and began typing his initial report for the attack on the government building. He needed to get the sequence of events and times written down before they became lost in the pile of notes.

Blake had typed several pages of his report when Sergeant McGuire knocked on the door to his office.

"Sorry to bug you. Do you have a minute?"

"Sure, what's up?"

"One of the groups was able to check John's last known address. His wife was home, and she said that he hasn't been home in two days. She said that John told her he was going out of town for work. The detective said that it appeared as though his wife was telling the truth."

"Hmm, did his employer say when he was last at work?"

"That's where it gets interesting. They went to his work and supposedly he hasn't been to work at all this week. John called them last Friday and said that he had a family emergency. He used vacation days to take this entire week off. He also told them that he'll call later in the week to let them know when he'd be returning."

"Wow, that's a pretty big coincidence. Has anyone been able to check into John's background?"

"Yeah, it looks like just a few minor run-ins with law enforcement. He was arrested for domestic battery against his first wife. The case was dropped after his wife declined to have the case prosecuted. He also has a DUI arrest from a few years ago. He eventually pled guilty to the DUI, but for some reason he didn't lose his driver's license during the conviction. Other than that, his record is clean."

"Does he have any known associates?"

"We weren't able to dig anything up. Several of the UCs are working their informants to see if they can come up with anything. There is confirmation that Robert and John were hanging out together for the past few months at the Legend. This may have garnered them a connection into this organized crime group."

"Well, that's definitely great news. Were they able to get John's cell phone number?"

"His wife reluctantly gave up the cell phone number. I wanted to see if you could send in an exigent circumstances request to his cell phone carrier to see if we can locate his whereabouts." Sergeant McGuire handed Blake a piece of paper that had John's cell phone number and carrier listed in black ink.

"Sure, I'll get that form e-mailed to the cell phone carrier right away. I'm curious to see where the GPS coordinates will show his phone to be."

Blake opened up the file containing the proper form and he filled out the required information. He searched through his e-mail contact list until he located the e-mail address for John's cell phone carrier. He attached the exigent circumstances form and attached it to an e-mail, which he addressed to the cell phone carrier. Blake hit the send button and jotted down the time he submitted the request.

"If his cell phone is pinging in the same area as Robert's, then we'll have some pretty good circumstantial evidence that these guys are, in fact, working together," Sergeant McGuire added. "It'll probably be enough to drag these guys in for questioning."

"By the sounds of it, it's not going to be easy to pick them up if they are staying on that compound in Riverside County. We'll have to wait until the meeting this afternoon to decide on a plan of action."

❦

Meanwhile, Garcia had returned to the government center's surveillance room with Chief Betts to review the remaining surveillance video from the day before the attack.

"I bet there is a good chance that these guys had a dry run before they actually went through with their plan," Garcia thought aloud. "The suspects were very calm and collected when they entered the government center yesterday morning before the attack. If I was planning on doing something like this, I would want to make sure everything went smoothly before I initiated the final plan."

"I'll start the video recording on Monday morning before the attack. Maybe we'll see these guys enter and we can get a better look at their faces."

The chief entered the date and time into the surveillance system. The video started out just before the government center opened the day before the attack.

After watching the video play for several minutes, it was obvious that the suspects had used the day to gather surveillance as to the exact operations of the government center. All of the suspects had entered the building at approximately the same time they entered on the day of the attack. They were all wearing the same clothing they wore during the attack. The suspects even went into the same bathrooms, apparently to make sure everything was going to work as planned.

Garcia used his cell phone and called one of the detectives scouring the building for any clues. He filled the detective in on the dry run that had occurred the day before the attack.

They continued watching the remaining surveillance footage and weren't able to gain any additional information. Chief Betts downloaded the surveillance footage onto a DVD so it could be secured into evidence.

Garcia returned to the investigations division and prepared the new surveillance footage to be sent to the RCTC for analysis. He completed the proper forms and submitted a file containing the surveillance footage through an e-mail.

Garcia checked his inbox and he still hadn't received a response from the initial inquiry he had sent to the RCTC yesterday.

The sun was out and a slight breeze could be felt across his face. The temperatures were expected to reach into the low eighties, and Blake was relieved to be conducting his portion of the investigation in an air-conditioned environment. Wearing a suit coat and dress clothes in this weather definitely wasn't something he wanted to be doing, he thought.

The two-hour car ride up to Riverside County was uneventful. They stopped and grabbed a bite to eat at a little roadside diner and continued on their way.

They had arrived at the Riverside County Sheriff's Office at 12:47 p.m. They entered the main lobby of the sheriff's office and were met by the receptionist, who was seated behind a small, sliding-glass window.

"We're here to meet with Sergeant Shaw," Blake said, showing his badge to the receptionist.

"Okay, I'll give him a call, and he'll be up in a few minutes. If you guys would like, there are a few seats over there," the receptionist said, pointing towards several metal chairs that sat in the corner.

"Thank you, ma'am," Blake said as they turned around and walked away from the window.

Garcia took a seat in the chairs, and Blake decided to remain standing. Blake looked at the display cases that were at the other end of the lobby. Apparently, the sheriff's department participated in fundraising for Special Olympics and had participated in several charity softball tournaments, as there were several trophies sitting in the display case.

The second display case was filled with statistics from within the sheriff's department. The number of police calls were each broken down into separate categories. Traffic accident statistics were also included in the display. Their department seemed to pride itself on traffic safety and had won several awards from various traffic safety groups.

As they continued looking around the lobby, the door near the receptionist opened and Sergeant Shaw held the door open for them. He was dressed in brown pants and a brown uniform shirt, which happened to be the standard uniform for sheriff's departments around the entire state of Michigan. The departments patch adorned each of his shoulders and chevrons, signifying his sergeant status in the department, were sewn onto his sleeves, just below the department's patch. He was a heavyset man with a balding head and a thick mustache. Blake thought he resembled something out of an old western movie.

"Hello, I'm Sergeant Shaw," the sergeant said, striking out his massive right hand.

"Hello, this is Detective Garcia, and I'm Detective Talbot," Blake said, and they shook hands.

"If you guys follow me this way, we can go over all the details of our past cases involving this property you were inquiring about."

They entered into a roll call room and took a seat at one of the small tables. Sergeant Shaw went through all of the intelligence information that their office was able to obtain over the past few years.

After they had looked through all of the information, Blake and Garcia left the sheriff's office and drove back to Humble County.

Terror from Within

On Thursday, Blake returned to the Humble County Sheriff's Office at 7:00 a.m. to continue the investigation.

He hadn't even had a chance to touch any of his other cases. For the time being, they were going to have to wait until this case could be wrapped up.

After attending the morning intelligence briefing, Blake returned to his office and checked his e-mails. Then he placed a phone call to the State's Attorney's Office. He briefed one of the assistant state's attorneys on the status of his investigation, regarding Robert entering the government center after hours and without permission. The ASA approved charges for criminal trespass to government-owned property. The ASA wanted Blake to speak with Robert before he would consider charging him with any further criminal acts. Blake thanked them for their time and hung up the phone.

He completed the criminal complaint and warrant paperwork. Blake went over to the SA's office and met with an associate judge, who issued the warrant of arrest for Robert.

Blake turned the paperwork over to the Circuit Clerk's Office, which generated a courtroom case number for the warrant.

After the case number for the court system was generated, Blake had the warrant entered into the law enforcement database. Now, if a law enforcement officer had contact with Robert, they could run him through the database and they would find out that he had an outstanding warrant out of Humble County. The warrant was extraditable in the entire state of Michigan, and this would help if Robert was at the property in Riverside County.

Chapter 21
Belcher, MI

On Friday, the investigation took a break to honor the officers who had paid the ultimate price while performing the job they all loved.

There were police cars from as far away as Pennsylvania and Minnesota filling the parking lots of the local hotels, as officers arrived to attend the services for their fallen brothers.

The visitation for the three officers was at Walter's Funeral Home in Belcher. Mourners began lining up at 5:00 a.m. for the viewing, which was set to begin at 9:00 a.m. By the time the actual viewing began, the line was approaching ten thousand people and it stretched for several blocks. The governor and several politicians from throughout Michigan had arrived to honor the fallen officers.

This case had led the local and national news since the incident first occurred; there were many federal and local law enforcement agencies on hand to provide security for the visitation. A screening center was erected at the entrance to the funeral home and everyone was searched prior to entering. Snipers could be seen on nearby rooftops, and several blocks around the funeral home were closed down to vehicular traffic.

Craig L'Esperance

A staging area for news media was set up across the street from the funeral home, and this allowed the reporters easy access to the mourners.

Blake attended the visitation with the rest of the investigators from the sheriff's office. They waited in line for five hours before finally reaching the entrance to the funeral home. The investigators all entered the funeral home together and were allowed several minutes alone with the families of the fallen officers.

By the time they left the funeral home, there wasn't a dry eye left in the group. Everyone wanted to get home and squeeze his or her loved ones as a reminder to how quickly life can change.

❧

On Saturday morning, tens of thousands of mourners gathered in the area of St. Mary's Catholic Church in Belcher to pay their final respects to the officers.

Prior to the funeral service, as each casket was brought to the church, fellow police officers stood silently along the road leading to the church in a solemn salute.

Before the funeral service began, a lone bagpiper played an excellent rendition of "Amazing Grace" that brought tears to the eyes of everyone who was able to witness the performance firsthand.

Only a fraction of those in attendance were able to be seated inside the church once the funeral services began. The remaining attendees watched the service at the Belcher High School gymnasium via a remote video feed.

The investigators working on the case were assigned seats in the front rows of the sanctuary.

The speakers at the memorial service included Sheriff Calhoun, the chief of the Three Forks Police Department, and several relatives of the slain officers.

After the service, a police honor guard fired off a three-volley rifle salute. Then, each of the slain officers' spouses were provided a folded United States Flag, which had previously been draped over their coffins.

The services concluded, and a funeral procession left the funeral home and traveled under a large American flag suspended between two fire trucks. The procession, including over five hundred police cars, weaved its way through downtown Belcher and to a local cemetery.

After the funeral services, a reception was held at the cafeteria of the Belcher High School. Blake spent the afternoon at the high school with countless other police officers, reminiscing about the good times he had with the fallen officers.

Blake left the high school just after 3:30 p.m. and drove home. He parked in the garage and went inside the house. Maria and the children were playing in the living room. He embraced each one of them and told them that he loved them. The events of the past week were emotionally catching up with him. In this line of work, there weren't any guarantees that you'd return from your tour of duty, and this struck a chord with Blake as he thought about not being there for his family.

The entire investigation for the case had been halted for the weekend to allow everyone to pay tribute to the fallen officers and their families. Blake needed these two days to recharge his batteries after a mentally grueling week.

He took time to play with his children around the house, and they walked up to the park to use the swing set, allowing Maria a break from the children.

"How about we take the night off of cooking a meal and go out to eat?" Blake asked when he returned from the park.

"That would be perfectly fine with me," Maria said from where she lay on the couch. "Any ideas on where we should go?"

"Let's try that Italian place on Grand River, just east of Three Forks."

"Sounds good; I will jump into the shower real quick and then I'll be ready to go." Maria left the living room and disappeared into the bathroom to take a shower.

They left their house a half hour later and arrived at the Italian restaurant in time to beat the evening dinner rush. They were able to spend the remainder of the evening enjoying each other's companionship.

Chapter 22
Three Forks, MI

Over the course of the next few weeks, there weren't any major developments in the investigation. The RCTC had been able to review the surveillance footage and they explained that the angle of the security cameras didn't allow for a positive identification with their facial recognition software.

The government center had reopened just over a week after the attack with beefed-up security in and around the building. Chief Betts had the surveillance cameras all lowered to offer a better view of everyone inside of the building. For the first few days after the building reopened, a police K-9 officer was stationed at the two main entrances to sniff out each and every package or bag that entered the building.

Chief Betts was in the planning stages of implementing a new innovative detection system at the two main entrances. Electronic keycard access was installed on each and every exterior door of the government center. This addition allowed Chief Betts and his staff the ability to monitor anyone who entered and exited the building at any time. That way, if an employee was fired and for some reason hadn't turned in his or her electronic keycard, the keycard could be deactivated and wouldn't allow access into the building.

A local contractor worked day and night on the damaged portion of the building and was able to have everything repaired before the building was reopened. The brick columns that were separated by large glass windows had to be replaced because they were blown out during the explosion. The exterior windows surrounding the columns were replaced as well. Several interior brick walls near the blast were replaced and the restrooms were completely remodeled.

A few days after the attack, several hundred mourners attended a ceremony outside of the government center where three trees were planted in memory of the three officers who paid the ultimate price with their lives. A small memorial garden and a reflection pond were set up in the middle of the three trees.

The normal cases continued to flow into the detective bureau for follow-up investigation. However, the top priority was still focused on the attack. For the most part, the citizens whose cases needed follow-up investigation were sympathetic to the events of the previous few weeks.

One morning, Blake was in his office when his telephone rang. He glanced at the caller ID and thought about not answering it, as he didn't recognize the number displayed on the screen. He finally decided to pick up the phone after the third ring.

"Detective Talbot," Blake said into the receiver.

"Detective Talbot, it's Sergeant Shaw from the Riverside County Sheriff's Department; do you have a few minutes?"

"Sure, how's everything going?"

Terror from Within

Blake had been in continual contact with Sergeant Shaw over the past few weeks. Surveillance was still set up in the area where the suspects were possibly hiding out. The surveillance units still hadn't been able to get close enough to monitor the activities at the property of the suspected attackers.

"You're never going to believe what just happened," Sergeant Shaw said.

Blake could sense the excitement in his voice.

"Go ahead."

"I was sitting in the office this morning, and in walks Mr. Robert Whitlock." The sergeant paused for a few seconds to let his words sink in before continuing. "He was in pretty rough shape when he came in. He said he's willing to speak with you in regards to this entire situation. When can you make it up here?"

"I'll fill in my sergeant and I'll make arrangements to leave the office right away. Has he said anything to you guys about what happened in the attack?"

"Not really; we're just trying to stall him until you can get here. Since the incident happened in your jurisdiction, I figured you guys would like to have the first shot at interviewing him."

"I really appreciate the phone call. I'll call you as soon as I'm in my car so you know when to expect us. In the meantime, if he begins to talk about the attack, could you please have someone take notes?"

"I can do that. I'll wait to hear back from you."

"Thanks a million," Blake said, quickly placing the receiver down.

Blake left his office and hurried down the hallway towards Sergeant McGuire's office. McGuire was sitting behind his desk and reading a stack of paperwork in front of him when Blake barged into his office.

"Sarge, do you have a minute real quick?" Blake said, a smile spreading across his face.

Sergeant McGuire could tell something was up, as Blake usually knocked on the door and waited to be acknowledged before interrupting him.

"What's up?"

"Is Lieutenant Young in his office?"

"I think so, why?"

"I need to fill you both in on a major development on our case."

They both left Sergeant McGuire's office, crossed the hallway, and stuck their heads into Lieutenant Young's office. Lieutenant Young was on the phone and he looked up to see both of their heads poking through his doorway. Lieutenant Young ended his phone conversation and hung up his phone. Sergeant McGuire and Blake each took a seat in the chairs across the desk from the lieutenant.

"What can I do for you?" Lieutenant Young asked, looking directly at Blake.

"I just received a telephone call from Sergeant Shaw at the Riverside County Sheriff's Department. He was in his office this morning when a weary-looking Robert Whitlock entered. Robert told them that he was willing to talk to one of our detectives about the attack on the government building."

Lieutenant Young could barely believe what he was hearing. "No shit—you're serious?"

"Yeah, I couldn't believe it, either. I wanted to see who was interested in making a road trip up to Riverside County to speak with Mr. Whitlock."

Sergeant McGuire interrupted. "Lieutenant, I think we should have a few guys drive up there in case we have more leads that need to be followed up."

"I'll head up there along with whoever else is available," Blake added.

"Blake, you and Garcia can head up there in one car. I'll drive up there with Sergeant McGuire in a separate car. I'd like to see firsthand what this guy has to say. We'll leave everyone else in the office to handle anything that comes in while we are gone."

"All right; I'll grab my case file and my laptop computer and I'll be ready to go. Let me check with Garcia to make sure he's available."

The lieutenant was still shaking his head in disbelief as Blake left his office in search of Garcia.

Blake checked Garcia's office and his lights were turned off. He flipped open his cell phone and scrolled through the contacts. He pressed the send button when he reached Garcia's telephone number.

Garcia picked up his phone after two rings.

"Garcia."

"Hey, do you have a second?"

"Sure, go ahead."

"We just got an important tip on our big case. I need you to head up to Riverside County with me."

"What's happening?"

"I'll fill you in on the way up there. How long will it take for you to get back in the office?"

"I'll be there in five minutes. I'm just pulling up to the gas pumps right now."

"Okay. I'll meet you out back. I'll drive my car up there."

Blake closed his phone and hurried back to his office. He grabbed the case file along with his laptop computer. He left the office and walked out the back door of the government center.

He crossed the parking lot and reached his unmarked squad car. Garcia was just pulling into the parking lot as Blake got into his car. Garcia parked his car several parking spaces away and jumped into the passenger seat of Blake's car.

"The suspense is killing me. What's going on?"

Blake put the car into drive and slowly pulled out of the parking space.

"What's your rush? We have a long car ride ahead of us," Blake said sarcastically, glancing over at Garcia.

Garcia usually didn't mind playing practical jokes on people, but he didn't seem to be in the mood to joke around.

"Geez, can't take a joke?" Blake added as he pulled out of the parking lot and onto Grand River Avenue. "I received a phone call from the sergeant in Riverside County this morning," Blake said, and went on to explain the details of the telephone call.

When he finished, Garcia was dumbfounded. "What are the chances of this happening? I mean, why in the world would Robert all of a sudden show up at the sheriff's department and want to give everything up?"

"Your guess is as good as mine at this point. We'll just have to see what he has to say. They are currently detaining him on our initial warrant until we can get there to interview him."

Blake made a quick phone call to the Riverside County Sheriff's Department and let the sergeant know that they were on the way to meet with Robert.

As they continued driving, Blake and Garcia tossed around potential ideas as to why Robert was suddenly willing to provide a statement. Maybe he didn't want to be on the run any longer, or maybe he was feeling remorseful for his actions, they thought.

They pulled into the parking lot at the Riverside County Sheriff's Department just after 11:00 a.m. Blake parked in the front lot and entered through a door labeled for the sheriff's department. Blake approached the receptionist and provided her with his business card. He explained the reason for their arrival and that he would like to speak with Sergeant Shaw. The receptionist told them she would have the sergeant meet them in a minute.

As they grabbed a seat in the corner of the lobby, Blake placed a phone call to Lieutenant Young.

"Hey, lieutenant, we're waiting to be let into the sheriff's department. I wanted to see if you wanted us to wait for you before we begin interviewing Robert."

"We'll be there in fifteen minutes. If you get a chance to start interviewing him before we get there, then go ahead and begin."

Blake was looking at the door near the receptionist as it opened.

"It looks like we're heading in there right now. I'll talk to you more when you guys get here."

"Sounds good; see you in a bit."

Blake saw Sergeant Shaw standing in the doorway, motioning for them to follow him into the office. Blake and Garcia jumped to their feet and entered into the office as Sergeant Shaw held the door open for them.

"Good morning, guys," the sergeant said, leading them down the hallway to their roll call room.

"Good morning. Thanks for giving us a call right away. This could definitely turn out to be the biggest break we have so far in the investigation," Blake said.

As they entered the roll call room, Blake noticed a television sitting in the corner that was split into two screens. The top screen showed a male sitting in one of their interview rooms.

They took seats near the television and Sergeant Shaw went over what had transpired earlier in the morning. He explained how Robert had walked into the lobby of the sheriff's department just after 7:00 a.m. Robert had told the supervisor who was on desk duty at the time, who he was, and why he needed to speak with an officer. His facial hair was long and starting to gray. He didn't resemble the picture that was floating around the sheriff's office. Once the supervisor determined what was going on, he made the proper notifications.

"Is your AV system already set up so we can record our interview with Robert?" Blake asked as he looked at the television screen.

"Yeah, we still have a VHS system, but it works fine. We can start the recording whenever you would like."

"If you could start it right now, that would be great. I've got my case file and we're ready to interview him, if that's fine with you."

Sergeant Shaw leaned over and pressed the record button on the machine. "Go right ahead, I'll monitor the interview to make sure you guys don't need anything."

"Thanks. My two commanders are en route up here to see what this guy has to say. If you could fill them in on the progress of the interview once they arrive, that would be tremendous."

"Not a problem at all."

With that, Blake and Garcia stood up and left the roll call room. The sergeant led them down the carpeted hallway and around the corner before stopping in front of a door labeled interview room number one.

The sergeant looked up at Blake and asked, "Do you guys need anything prior to starting the interview? Would you like any water or coffee?"

Garcia looked over at Blake. "I'm okay right now; thanks for the offer."

"Do you guys have a gun locker where we can secure our guns?" Garcia asked as he motioned towards his firearm.

"Yeah, it's right over here," Sergeant Shaw said, leading them into a room located down the hallway.

Blake and Garcia both locked up their guns and ammunition prior to beginning the interview. Blake took a deep breath and he opened the door to the interview room and entered, followed by Garcia, who shut the door behind them. The interview room was similar to the one at their department. There was a small table sitting in the corner of the room. There happened to be one empty chair near the table and one empty chair in the corner of the room.

"Are you Robert?"

"Yes," Robert said as he glanced up at the two detectives who had entered the room.

"This is Detective Garcia," Blake said, pointing towards Garcia. "My name is Detective Talbot, and we both work for the Humble County Sheriff's Department."

Blake took a seat near Robert, and Garcia sat down in the empty chair in the corner.

"It's my understanding that you have some information that will be beneficial to us in one of our investigations; is that true?" Garcia asked.

"I have a few things that I need to get off my mind. First off, I wanted to see if there is a possibility that I can work out a deal by giving you guys some information."

"What kind of deal are you looking to get?" Blake said, looking directly into Robert's eyes.

"I'm just looking for leniency on a few things when this case goes to court."

Blake glanced quickly over at Garcia and then turned towards Robert. "I can't make any promises because I don't know what kind of information you have. We are willing to talk with our SA's office prior to filing charges and let them know that you were cooperative. First, since you are currently in custody, let me read you your Miranda Warnings."

Blake pulled out a pre-printed form and read Robert his Miranda Warnings. After he was done, he asked Robert to place his initials next to each warning and to sign at the bottom of the form, which indicated that he understood the warnings. Robert signed in the appropriate locations and slid the form back across the table to Blake. Blake completed the date and time portion at the bottom of the form.

Robert was still dressed in the clothes he had walked in with. Just to be on the safe side, Blake had Robert stand up so he could pat him down to make sure he didn't have any weapons or contraband on him. After he patted him down, they both took a seat.

"What kind of information do you have for us?" Blake asked, sitting back in his chair.

"Where would you like me to start?"

"Well, since we haven't discussed any portion of what case you're talking about, how about you start from the beginning."

Robert started out by detailing his childhood. He explained that he wanted to paint a picture of his upbringing and how he turned his life around to become a productive member of society so they didn't think he was a complete piece of shit.

He told them how he was raised in a seedy one-bedroom apartment in downtown Lansing. He described how the stairway leading to the apartment was always covered in used condoms and broken glass. He talked about how the walls inside of the apartment were stained from years of cigarette smoke and how it always smelled like a dirty diaper. He paused for a second, and then continued by tell them how his siblings all shared a twin mattress that sat in the corner of the living room. The mattresses rarely had sheets on them, and their two cats frequently used them for their litter box. This wasn't the cats' fault, as they were never provided a litter box to use. He explained how the cats would often nibble on old pizza crust so they wouldn't starve to death. Robert said the kitchen cupboards were always empty, except for an occasional box of stale Rice Krispies. The refrigerator rivaled the cupboards and usually only held a case of Old Style and a half-empty gallon of milk. Robert's mother always insisted that they not waste milk, and when the children were done eating cereal, they dumped their leftover milk, including soggy cereal pieces, back into the gallon container. To his mother, this was better than buying a new gallon of milk every week, which the family didn't have money for. Robert told them how the bathroom was always littered with used syringe wrappers, and open needles lay strewn about the bathroom. It was rare for him to see a roll of toilet paper or bar of soap in the bathroom.

Robert filled them in on how, when he was twelve years old, his father overdosed on heroin and died in their apartment. This left his mother with five children to raise, even though she never worked outside of the home.

Robert continued detailing his previous problems by telling them about the falling out with his wife within the past year. He told them about how this drove him to drink heavily. He told them how he began neglecting his children and was soon trapped in a world he had promised himself that he'd never get sucked into.

"I was becoming my own worst nightmare. I had been kicked out of my own house and was not even allowed to see my own children. I was unable to control my alcohol consumption and, in a way, I was becoming my father, who was never able to control this gripping disease," Robert said, wiping a tear away from his eye.

Throughout this entire story, Blake could tell it was coming from Robert's heart, and he actually seemed devastated by his actions and his inability to provide for his family. In a way, Blake felt sorry for Robert. It seemed like he had straightened his life around for a short period of time before the alcohol took control and he spiraled out of control.

"Tell us what happened after your wife filed for the OP and divorce," Garcia said, leaning forward and placing his elbows on his knees.

Robert told them about his frequent trips to the Legend. He filled them in on how he ran into a guy named John Gibson, who he had lost contact with over the last several years. He said that John was connected with a guy by the name of Samuel Jenson, who was slinging quite a bit of dope out of the bar. Robert said that one day he was propositioned to join their crew, and he couldn't pass it up with his recent layoff from his job as a maintenance worker for Humble County.

Robert gave the detectives the details of the crime spree he had taken part in, which included some cases that Blake still had open and sitting on his desk back at the office.

Blake couldn't believe his luck that this case was going beyond the scope of the attack on the government center. This had potential to crack a major criminal enterprise that had been operating in the Humble County area. Blake knew that this was probably only the tip of the iceberg.

Chapter 23
Riverside County, MI

Sam rolled over and slowly opened his eyes as rays of the morning's sunlight were peaking through the wooden blinds in his bedroom. He looked at the alarm clock that was sitting on the nightstand beside the bed. It was 9:22 a.m., and he couldn't remember the last time he had slept in that late.

He swung his feet over the side of the bed and reached for a pair of shorts. He slid them on before standing up and rummaging through a pile of dirty clothes in search of a t-shirt to wear. Sam chose a gray shirt that was sitting near the bottom of the pile. The shirt had probably been sitting on the floor for several weeks, but Sam didn't care one bit. He was his own boss and he could do whatever he felt like.

Sam left his bedroom and walked down the hallway before descending the stairs to the main floor. Once he reached the kitchen, he could tell that it was going to be another perfect day out on the ranch.

He poured himself a bowl of cereal and, as he ate his breakfast, he could see out the back sliding-glass door. There were several guys working on repairing one of the barns that had been neglected throughout the years. They were in the process of a complete rehab on the barn and once it was finished, they would be able to fit at least a dozen vehicles inside. A new coat of red paint was applied to the barn less than a week ago.

When he was done, he placed the bowl in the sink and returned the milk to the refrigerator. Sam thought about how things had changed on the ranch since the bureaucrats decided they were going to cut power to the property. Fortunately, they had already equipped the building to run on several large industrial-sized generators. They had installed large gasoline storage tanks in several of the barns that would allow them enough fuel to last for several years if they used it sparsely.

Sam returned to his bedroom and took off his shorts. He put on a pair of dirty blue jeans. Then he left the bedroom, shutting the door behind him. He walked downstairs and pulled on a rugged pair of leather boots. He left out the side door and went to check on the progress in the barn. Sam arrived at the barn and checked out the projects that were already in the works. Two guys were working on shoring up the header above the large roll-up garage door.

Guzman was outside of the barn, working on one of the wood-burning stoves. Sam walked over to him. "Have you seen Robert this morning?" Sam said with a puzzled look on his face.

"Now that you mention it, I haven't seen him at all. Are you sure he wasn't still sleeping?" Guzman said, briefly glancing around the barn.

"I didn't check his room. I just figured he was out here working on the barn. I'll have to run inside and see if he's still sleeping."

Sam turned around and walked back up to the house. It was odd for Robert to be the last one out of bed. He was

Terror from Within

usually eagerly running around and willing to help with any project that needed to be finished. Sam was beginning to like the work ethic that Robert showed since he had taken up residency on the ranch.

Sam climbed the steps up to the side door and pulled open the screen door. He walked across the hardwood floor and took the stairs two at a time. He reached the door to Robert's bedroom and paused to listen for a second. After hearing nothing but silence, Sam turned the knob and slowly slid the door open. At first glance, it appeared as though Robert was still sleeping in bed and everything in the room was neat and tidy. Sam walked across the small bedroom and peaked over the edge of the covers. He reached forward and pulled the covers of the blanket back and, to his to amazement, Robert wasn't in the bed. In his place were several pillows and blankets that were made to look like someone was sleeping in the bed.

Sam bolted out of the room and descended the stairs in two giant leaps. He ran out the side door and continued until he reached the barn.

"I need everyone here now!" Sam yelled as he began pacing back and forth across the dirt driveway.

Three guys appeared out of the barn and stood just outside of the door. Guzman left the wood-burning stove and joined the crew at the front of the barn.

"What's up?" Guzman said, trying to decipher what was wrong. Then he realized that Sam had left a few minutes ago to look for Robert.

"Where in the hell is Robert?" Sam said, and without allowing anyone a chance to respond, he flew into a tirade. "I want every one of you to start tearing this place apart for any signs of him. He better not have left sometime during the night. When was the last time anyone saw him?" Sam's face became flushed red with anger.

Guzman looked around and then said, "I haven't seen him since last night when I went to bed."

Nobody else said anything, as they hadn't seen or heard from Robert, either. They didn't waste any time standing around looking for an answer. Three of the guys returned to the barn and jumped into two separate pickup trucks. They spun the trucks tires and sped off as dust filled the air.

Sam and Guzman each got onto separate ATVs and rode towards the back of the property. There was a crude two-rut path around the entire property. The trucks took the path around the property as the ATVs took the rough terrain through the middle of the property.

They all searched in and around the property, and the initial search turned up no signs of Robert. Sam's fears began mounting as he continued searching for any indication that Robert had left on foot through the dense prairie grass. Every portion of trampled grass they searched only turned up signs of white tail deer.

Sam picked up his cell phone and thought about calling Robert's phone to see where he was. After thinking about it for a few seconds, Sam decided against making that phone call. If Robert had fled the area, he was probably going directly to the police, Sam thought. He needed some time to think about what to do next. In the back of his mind, Sam always knew there was a possibility that Robert would decide he had had enough and would leave the crew.

Terror from Within

Sam pulled out his portable two-way radio and called in to check the status of the others who were still searching. The two trucks, which had portable radios mounted in them, both indicated that they hadn't located any signs of Robert. Sam advised them to return to the barn, and they would discuss what the next plan of action would be.

About fifteen minutes later, the entire group was gathered back in front of the barn. The mid morning sun was beginning to make things rather uncomfortable, as they pondered what their possible options were.

Sam immediately ruled out the possibility of leaving the property in search of Robert. For all they knew, the police had already set up a perimeter and were lying in wait for someone to leave the property. Sam decided that they would lay low for a while before they decided to try to leave the property. The impromptu meeting ended a short time later, and everyone resumed his or her previous tasks.

Sam returned to the house and entered through the side door. He didn't bother to take off his shoes as he continued across the kitchen and walked into the living room.

Sam rolled back a rug that was spread across the living room floor. Under the rug was a secret hatch that led down to the basement. The basement wasn't in the original house plans, and there was only a crawl space when they had purchased the house. Over the past several years, the guys had spent countless hours digging out the basement by hand. They had rigged up a pulley system to haul the dirt out of a newly constructed basement window. The dirt was hauled to different parts of the property and used as fill. After the project was complete, the basement had been turned into a quasi bomb shelter. It was complete with four-foot thick, reinforced concrete. One of the rooms had a year's supply of food and a ventilation system that would allow anyone plenty of time to stay cooped up in the room.

In the second room, a sophisticated surveillance system was connected wirelessly to numerous infrared cameras situated around the property. From this room, Sam had the ability to manipulate the cameras to see what was going on around the property. A DVR was linked to the system and allowed the surveillance video to be stored for up to a month.

Sam climbed down a wooden ladder that led into the basement. He crossed the small entryway and entered the surveillance room. He sat down on an oak stool in front of one of the monitors. He shook the mouse, and the screen came to life. Sixteen different boxes were visible on the screen, and each box represented a different camera. Sam moved the mouse to the bottom of the screen and entered in the last time anyone saw Robert on the property. He pressed play and watched each camera for any signs of Robert leaving the house.

As the video reached 3:41 a.m., Sam could see movement on the main floor of the house. There weren't any lights on inside, but with the IR cameras he could clearly see Robert walking towards the side door. The door opened very slowly, and then Robert slipped out the door, closing it behind him.

One of the surveillance cameras outside picked up a glimpse of Robert as he darted between two of the barns. After watching the video, Sam had a hunch that Robert had taken one of the well-worn paths in the prairie grass towards the back of the property. Shit, Sam thought as he slammed his fist down on the table next to the monitor.

"How was he able to sneak out without waking anyone up?" Sam said aloud as he stood up from the stool.

He left the room and climbed back up the ladder. He replaced the hidden door and slid the rug back into place.

Chapter 24

"So, how is it that you ran with these guys during their crime spree, and then they somehow managed to rope you into setting them up with the ability to attack the Humble County Government Center?" Blake said as they continued interviewing Robert.

"I didn't help them out with the attack on the government center, I promise," Robert said, rubbing his hands together.

Blake slammed his stack of paperwork on the table. "Do you really believe that I'm falling for your bullshit? I may have been born at night, but it definitely wasn't last night. Now you already have major issues for all the burglaries you guys did. If you think I'm not going to hammer you to the wall for those cases, then you're mistaken, because I will. Do you really want to spend the next ten years locked up in prison? I suggest that you cut the crap and give us only what actually happened." Blake was starting to lose his temper.

"I promise you I didn't want to help them out at all. I already admitted to helping them with their burglaries, and we never hurt anyone. As these months went along, things slowly started getting out of hand. I really think it had to do with Sam getting back into using cocaine. At first, he was level headed and only sold cocaine at the Legend. Then, as time progressed, he got hooked on cocaine himself. The short-term effects, namely the increased energy, really seemed to fuel his ego. He began regularly using cocaine to help sustain longer periods of activity, which usually included us casing a house or actually breaking into houses. Sam would go days without eating, and I think after a few weeks, he was hooked. Our productivity, if that's what you want to call it, went through the roof once he started taking the cocaine." Robert was looking directly at Blake as he continued. "Sam began using a half ounce of cocaine every day, and his behavior became extremely erratic and violent. He would regularly threaten to kill us if we ever ratted on him. He was paranoid that I was an undercover cop, and he patted me down for the first few weeks to make sure I wasn't wearing a wire."

Blake had heard enough about Sam's drug use, and it wasn't exactly what he was after. "You still didn't answer my question as to how you assisted them with the attack. Let me remind you that any question I ask, I already know the answers to."

"Sorry, I got sidetracked. We were hanging out at the Legend several weeks before the attack, and Sam gave me a proposition. He brought up the fact that I used to work for the county as a maintenance worker, and that he needed me to do him a huge favor. He went on to tell me how one of his buddies, Guzman, was locked up in the county jail, and he needed to get him out. Sam said that Guzman was being held without bond, and that I could help him with his plan. After he finished telling me about the plan, I told him that I really couldn't do what he wanted. He was pissed off and told me to meet him in one of the offices on the second floor of the Legend. I knew it wasn't the greatest idea, but at the time I didn't have any choice. So, I went upstairs and Sam followed closely behind me. Two other goons in the bar followed us upstairs as well. Once we got into the office, Sam hit me across the face with the back of his hand. He told me that I didn't have a choice but to help him out."

Robert shifted uneasily in his chair, and then rubbed his hands through his hair.

"Do you need a cigarette or something to drink?" Blake asked, hoping that it would ease Robert's nerves.

"I'd really like a cigarette, if you could get me one. Something to drink would be great; I'm thirsty."

"I'll be right back."

Garcia stayed in his chair as Blake quickly left the interview room. Blake stopped in the AV room and saw that Lieutenant Young and Sergeant McGuire were already settled in and were watching the interview.

"Great job!" Lieutenant Young said as Blake walked into the room. "We got here just after you started the interview. I can't believe that these guys are tied into a lot of our open cases."

"Neither could I," Blake said, smiling. "I'm curious to see where he's going with his participation in the attack." Blake looked over at Sergeant Shaw, who was admiring the fine job that Blake was doing with the interview. "Is there any chance that we could let him have one cigarette?"

The sergeant shrugged his shoulders. "We don't really allow that, but this case can be an exception. I'll go see if I can get a cigarette from one of the patrol guys."

The sergeant got up from his chair and left the AV room in search of a cigarette.

"I'm going to let him keep going, and we'll see where he goes," Blake continued as he waited for the sergeant to return.

They continued making small talk about the interview until the sergeant returned with a can of Coke and a cigarette. Blake took the cigarette and Coke, along with an ashtray and a lighter, before he left the roll call room and returned to the interview room. Blake shut the door to the interview room and slid the ashtray across the table towards Robert. He placed the can of Coke next to the ashtray and then handed Robert the cigarette and lighter.

Robert lit the cigarette and took several long drags before he finally rested his right arm on the table just above the ashtray.

"So, what happened after Sam hit you and said you didn't have a choice but to assist him?" Blake exclaimed.

"He told me that he couldn't trust me anymore because I wasn't being a team player. Sam had pulled out a sheet of paper and told me that he knows where my soon-to-be ex-wife and kids live. He made it very clear that if I decided to go against his planned attack on the government building, then he'd harm my family." Robert shook his head slightly from side to side as his eyes started to tear up. "For as many problems as I've had with my wife, I still love her and the kids. I'd do anything to protect them from any harm." Robert placed his head into his hands and began to cry.

For the next minute or two, nobody said a word. Blake was letting the entire situation sink in for Robert.

Then Blake reached forward and gently touched Robert's shoulder. "I know how you feel when you said you'd do anything for your family. If I was in your shoes, I'd do the same thing. How did Sam force you to help them?"

Robert kept his face buried in his hands. "He knew that I still had some items left over from when I worked at the government center. I had made a mistake when I first met Sam by telling him I still had a spare key to get into the government center. Sam remembered me telling him about the spare key, and he explained how his plan included me entering the building and planting some weapons inside of several restrooms."

"I might be missing something, but we were able to watch the surveillance video of you entering the building the night before the attack and planting the guns," Garcia chimed in. "You were the only one to enter the building and you could have easily called the police from a phone inside of the government center and asked for assistance."

"That's the thing. Sam wired a small camera into the brim of my baseball hat, which included an audio feed. He was able to watch the video feed remotely from outside of the government building. As a precaution, he strapped a black bag to my back loaded with PETN. Sam added a remote detonation chord to the front of the backpack so I wouldn't be able to take it off without blowing myself to pieces."

Blake and Garcia could hardly believe what they had just heard. They both sat in silence, as Robert continued filling them in on the details.

"So, Sam and John drove me to the government center and we parked in the back parking lot. We waited in

Sam's SUV until the entire maintenance crew was gone for the evening. Then Sam wired up the explosive and placed the baseball hat on top of my head. He actually wished me luck and promised not to harm me as long as I planted everything where he wanted. I was dressed in one of my old maintenance uniforms, and nobody would have thought twice about seeing me inside of the building that late at night. I used my spare key and entered the back door by the loading docks. I hid several assault rifles inside of the trashcans in the restrooms. After I was done, I left the building and returned to Sam's SUV."

"Do you know where Sam got these explosives from?" Blake asked.

"I know they have a ton of illegal guns and explosives at their property not far from here. I'm sure that's where he got it from."

"Where did you guys go after you hid the guns in the building?"

"Sam drove up to their land where we had previously come from. In fact, it wasn't long before this incident that I was aware of this property and the major threat these guys actually could wreak on society. I was constantly monitored while on the ranch, as they would call it, and I wasn't allowed to leave at all. I heard Sam and several of the others talking about the details of the attack. Sam made it sound like it was a success and there was only one minor issue that had been resolved rather quickly."

"Is there anything else that you think would be beneficial to our investigation?" Blake asked, continuing to stare at Robert.

"Not that I can think of."

"I really appreciate your cooperation. I'm sure we'll need to talk with you again once we're able to go over all of the details of this case. As I'm sure you're already aware, you're currently being charged with criminal trespass to a government building. We need to tie up a few loose ends before we can proceed with trying to make contact with Sam and his cronies."

"I understand. I just want to warn you that these guys will stop at nothing to create an absolute bloodbath if you guys try to raid their property. They have enough guns, explosives, and surveillance to keep you guys from ruining their day."

Chapter 25

"As we had previously suspected, Robert left the house very early this morning," Sam told the rest of the guys once he returned outside. "There is only one reason he would sneak out of this place in the middle of the night. We're going to need to lay low for a while and see what happens. I don't want anyone leaving the property unless you first discuss it with me. Is that understood?"

Everyone nodded in agreement except Guzman, who was leaning up against the garage door of the barn. His tattooed and muscular arms were folded across his chest and he didn't even acknowledge Sam.

"Guzman, what the hell is your problem? Since when have you become such a hard-ass?"

Guzman stood for a moment without saying anything. He'd been through a lot recently and he wasn't about to let Sam run the show.

"Okay jack-ass, you pull off one job, and all of a sudden, everyone is supposed to become your little bitch. Well, I've had enough of your shit. If you continue acting like this, then I'm gonna have to bounce. I've helped you out a ton over the past few years."

By now, Sam had inched his way forward and was right in Guzman's face. Sam knew Guzman was right, but he wasn't about to drop it that easily. "Okay, and what makes you think our little stunt at the government building was such an easy hit? You ain't ever done anything that big, have ya? We all put our asses out on the line to help a brother out, and you don't even respect that."

"I'll admit that I've never taken on anything that big before. This doesn't mean that I never gave you information or assisted with your little games you were playing. If it wasn't for me, you wouldn't have been able to survive this long without getting caught."

Sam knew he was right. Guzman had bent over backwards to help with their burglary crew. He provided them with inside information that only secretary of state employees could provide. He was able to alert them every time their vehicle's license plates were run by any law enforcement agency. He provided them with fraudulent driver's licenses and license plates to help them complete their missions over the last few years.

"You're right, I may have gotten a little rough over the past few weeks, but you've got to understand what we're going through. We have elevated ourselves beyond the basic mom and pop bullshit. With that attack on the government building, we've opened ourselves up to a whole new level of scrutiny. Our days of running around under the radar of the police are over. All we've got left is our little slice of the America dream and we'll fight for this until we die. It won't be long before the cops get their little game plan together and try to disrupt our lives. It's now or never if we're going to try and defend ourselves." Sam looked up after he was done speaking and he could tell that Guzman was satisfied.

Terror from Within

A slight grin had formed across Guzman's face and he extended his right hand forward. Sam extended his right hand as well, and they both firmly shook hands. The rest of the guys just looked on in bewilderment at what they had just witnessed.

"What's the game plan going to be?" Guzman asked as he let go of Sam's right hand. "We don't have time to be standing around arguing."

They all returned to the house and discussed their plan of defense against a possible attempt by the police to swarm the property and take everyone into custody. They ate lunch and poured over their options. As lunch ended, their final plan had been established. The guys left the house and set up for their final stand.

Chapter 26

Blake and Garcia had left the interview room after speaking with Robert and were sitting in the roll call room when Sergeant McGuire and Lieutenant Young both entered the room.

The sergeant from Riverside County had re-handcuffed Robert and was waiting for one of their correctional officers to come and transport him down to the jail.

"We'll have to wait and see what the sergeant says when he returns," Lieutenant Young said as he unclipped his cell phone from his belt. "I'm going to place a call to representatives from the MSP, ATF, and FBI. I'll fill them in on the details of the interview. I'm sure they'll want to have a few guys present during our briefing. Our ops plan will definitely classify this case in the highest-risk category. We'll need to get input from all the agencies involved and see what our strategy will be."

Lieutenant Young scrolled through his phone and made several phone calls to update everyone on the case.

Sergeant Shaw returned to the roll call room as Lieutenant Young was finishing one of the phone calls.

"Sergeant, I'd like to get your input on this case. I've had time to glance over most of your previous run-ins with these guys. No matter which way you look at it, things don't look good for us," Lieutenant Young said with a concerned look.

"No, they really don't. These guys are the most sophisticated group we've ever had to deal with. Their firearms training seems to be top notch and they won't hesitate to murder one of our guys."

"I just placed calls into the MSP, ATF, and FBI. They've all previously assisted us with our investigation. It looks like we'll need to set up a briefing to update everyone on the case and get everyone's input on what our plan of attack will be. I'm suggesting that we get this meeting set up as soon as possible. Is there any way we could use your roll call room to hold the meeting?"

"While I was waiting for Robert to be picked up, I made a phone call to my boss. He relayed the information to the sheriff, and the sheriff said he'll be heading over here ASAP," Sergeant Shaw added.

Everyone went into planning mode for the next two hours as phone calls were made and everyone had a chance to send a representative to the meeting.

Sergeant Shaw began the process of obtaining a search warrant for the property where the suspects were hiding out. With assistance from Blake, he completed the search warrant paperwork and submitted it to their head SA for review. After the SA read over the affidavit and search warrant, they brought the paperwork before the on-call judge. The judge glanced over the paperwork and immediately issued a search warrant for the property.

Lieutenant Young ordered pizza for everyone from a local restaurant, and they were just finishing the pizza as the first few guys arrived for the briefing.

Terror from Within

Blake looked down at his watch just as it turned 4:02 p.m. He scanned the standing-room-only crowd as the intelligence briefing started. The federal agencies had sent several investigators each; the MSP had several detectives from the Belcher Post, as well as the Indian River Post. Sheriff Calhoun had made the trip up to the meeting along with Chief Betts from court security. The other remaining detectives from the Humble County Sheriff's Department had caravanned up to the meeting.

The United States Marshals Service (USMS) was called in from the active surveillance at the ranch to provide their expertise on planning high-risk suspect apprehension.

The meeting began with Lieutenant Young giving an overall briefing of the attack on the government center for those in attendance who didn't have all the details. He then briefly explained how the investigation led to the one-hundred-acre property in Riverside County. He thanked all of the agencies for their cooperation during the investigation and then opened the floor for discussion on how they should proceed.

The discussion continued for the next hour and a half. Many valid issues were brought up and addressed the best they could. Everyone in the room agreed that this group needed to be stopped as quickly and safely as possible. Because the information provided by Robert had the potential to go stale, if they waited too long to act, the plan was to go into action early the next morning. This time frame would allow everyone to have his or her equipment and manpower in place for the raid to occur at 3:00 a.m. sharp.

An issue that arose during the planning stages included how the different agencies were going to communicate with their separate radio frequencies. The federal agencies were using an 800 mhz radio system, as was the Humble County Sheriff's Office. The Riverside County Sheriff's Office was still using the old VHF radio frequency. Fortunately, the Riverside County Sheriff's Office was allowed to borrow enough portable radios from all of the local police agencies so everyone could communicate on the same channel.

The USMS brought in a large group of marshals, which included many local police officers who were part of the USMS task force from southeast Michigan. They also brought in two Bell Ranger helicopters to be used in the raid and staged them at the Riverside Municipal Airport, which was just down the road from the sheriff's department.

Conservation officers with the State of Michigan were able to bring in an entire fleet of low-profile boats that would be utilized in a ground assault via the Birch River that runs through the property.

It was agreed upon that nobody would speak about this case to anyone outside of his or her agencies. Due to the fact that Riverside County was relatively rural, there needed to be emphasis on keeping the local news media in the dark about the pending raid. If word got out about the feds arriving in town, the news would surely spread like wildfire. The last thing anyone needed was for Sam and his crew to be tipped off about when the raid was going to occur.

Terror from Within

As the briefing was winding down, Blake pulled up the weather forecast on his laptop computer. Throughout the remainder of the evening, the winds were going to be non-existent and there wasn't even the slightest chance for precipitation. This was good news for the operation because it allowed them to make use of the helicopters.

After the intelligence briefing was completed, everyone was given until 1:00 a.m. to allow each agency to gather any needed resources. The commanders from each agency were going to assemble to simulate a dry run of the ops plan in the training room at the Riverside County Sheriff's Office.

Robert was re-interviewed by several investigators to gather more specific information into potential hazards. He was able to provide useful information regarding where some of the cameras were set up. He advised them that all the suspects would be armed with a gun at all times. It was one of the main rules that Sam and his crew stood by, and that was to be able to protect yourself at all times. Robert wrote down a rough sketch of the property and included where some of the buildings were situated.

After all of the assets were in place and accounted for, many of the guys laid down to catch a quick nap. Most of them wouldn't be getting to sleep until the following night, and nobody was about to compromise one of the biggest operations in the history of the entire state.

At 1:00 a.m. the entire group assembled at the local high school. A wife of one of the deputies provided them with a key to the building so they could conduct their full briefing. The group had swelled to over one hundred federal and local law enforcement officers. The group was split into several different sections to provide the most coverage over the entire property.

After the initial assignments were given out, a team of snipers left the high school in search of a place to set up on the property. The team of ten snipers split up into two vehicles and left the parking lot in opposite directions. The plan was for them to approach the target property from the north and the west. Each sniper was dressed in camouflage, which would blend nicely into the local terrain. The team needed to get into place before anyone else so they could get eyes on the property to scope any potential dangers.

Each group was assigned a commander who would be situated at a command post back at the Riverside County Sheriff's Office. These commanders would work together to coordinate the entire raid. Once all units were in place, they were supposed to notify the command post to get clearance to continue with their assignments.

After the assignments were given, everyone broke from the meeting and assembled at their pre-determined locations.

The Humble County sheriff's investigators were assigned to provide perimeter containment to the property. They were told to make sure nobody entered or, more importantly, exited the property without the proper authority. Blake donned his tactical vest along with his ballistic helmet. He joined Garcia, Sergeant McGuire, Lieutenant Young, and the rest of their officers at the rear of the gymnasium. They were joined by several uniformed patrol officers from the MSP and other local agencies. Most of

Terror from Within

the guys were on the local SWAT team and knew the area around the property well.

Once everyone in their containment team was accounted for, they left the high school and positioned themselves so they were surrounding the entire property. Each officer was assigned to keep an eye on a hundred-yard section in either direction. Once everyone was in place, they radioed into their commander.

Officers from the Riverside County Sheriff's Office were split up and assigned to separate teams. Their expertise of the local land and roads provided an invaluable asset to each team.

The next team of approximately forty officers split into two, twenty-man teams. The first team caravanned to a park located on the Birch River, about a half mile north of the property. The second team traveled down a few two-track roads and parked near the Birch River, south of the property.

Once at their locations, each team unloaded the small boats and placed them in the river. According to the intelligence briefing, the river was about fifteen feet wide and was about five feet deep in the middle. The river flowed to the south at a very slow pace at this time of year because of the lack of any recent heavy rains. This would allow the team on the south side of the property a chance to make it up stream without much effort.

According to the topographical maps and satellite views, both groups needed to travel about a half mile to the middle of the property before disembarking the boats and climbing onto land. The intelligence briefing indicated the groups likely wouldn't encounter their first trouble until they hit land. The satellite views showed a large barn right near the river, which was most likely used to store equipment. They would need to keep several officers posted near the barn to make sure it wasn't occupied, as the remainder of the group continued towards the main buildings on the property. They needed to keep an eye on the barn until it was cleared so they weren't ambushed from behind.

Each boat was loaded with five officers, and the signal was given over the radio for the boats to begin silently moving towards the target property. As they moved along, they could hear updates coming into the command post from the snipers who were already in place. The snipers were reporting that everything appeared to be quiet from the main portion of the property. As the initial stages of the raid began, there were no reported problems.

Chapter 27

Sam was sound asleep in bed when his phone started buzzing on the nightstand next to him. Sam's phone never interrupted his sleep, and he quickly sat up in his bed. He tried to gather his thoughts as he reached forward and picked up his cell phone. He flipped the cell phone open, and his heart sank to the bottom of his stomach. On the screen he could see a live feed from one of his surveillance cameras. He sat there for a second and stared in disbelief. His alarm system had signaled a breach in one of the laser beams that ran across the river on the south side of his property. The camera located near the laser beam had come to life and now showed several boats migrating up the river. It was the way the guys were dressed and the manner in which they were moving that caused Sam the greatest concern. These guys seemed to be coming in waves and they weren't here for a picnic.

Holy shit, he thought as he pulled up his pants and grabbed his t-shirt, which was hanging on the back of his door. Sam yanked his bedroom door open and raced down the hallway. He was banging on the other bedroom doors as he ran past them.

"Get your asses up; we've got company!" Sam yelled at the top of his lungs. His heart was racing and he knew this wasn't going to be a false alarm.

As Sam reached the bottom of the stairs, he could hear doors starting to open from the second floor. He turned around and shouted up the stairs, "Hurry up, we've got a few minutes before this whole place is going to be surrounded by these bastards." Sam's phone buzzed again and he flipped it open for a second time. This time, he knew things were going to get ugly. The laser beam that ran across the river on the north side of the property had been tripped, and now another wave of heavily armed men was traveling south towards the middle of his property.

Sam had traveled up and down that river many times, and he knew it would be less than ten minutes before they all reached the middle of his property.

Sam was already in the living room and had the rug rolled back and the hidden door open just as the others appeared in the living room. The dogs had sensed there was a problem and followed Sam into the living room. He thought for a second and decided to let them come with them. He helped the dogs down the narrow ladder and they ran around the basement.

"Don't turn on any lights in case they have already surrounded the house."

One by one, each of them climbed down the narrow ladder and into the basement. Sam slid the carpet over the hole and then slid the hidden door closed. He moved the large bolts into place and the secret door was secured shut.

They all filed into the surveillance room to see what their next course of action would be. The monitors were on, and the only cameras that had been activated were the ones on the bank of the river. Nothing else appeared to be moving around the property. Sam knew that their options were limited at this point. He couldn't help but blame himself for not keeping a better eye on Robert when he was in the house. He knew that once Robert was gone, the police would likely act quickly on any information he may have provided them.

Sam reached over and flipped a switch on the wall. "This will at least temporarily disrupt their ability to communicate," Sam said as a smirk formed across his face. "The only way they are going to be effective in their mission is if they can have open lines of communication with each other." All cellular telephone and portable radio communication on the property was now being jammed.

Three more cameras became active as they sensed motion in the field of view. They could see the boats slowly pulling up to the banks of the river near one of the barns. The heavily armed officers hurried off the boats and spread out around the immediate area. Their guns were trained in every direction possible. Four of the officers could be seen tactically approaching the barn with their assault rifles drawn and aimed at the two doors. Sam could see that the officers all appeared to be wearing night-vision goggles and wouldn't have any trouble seeing without the aid of the flood light. As they came closer to the barn, a motion light turned on and the entire area in front of the service door was illuminated. This sent the officers scrambling to find the cover of darkness.

Sam and his crew continued watching as the remainder of the officers had disappeared out of view of the cameras and were headed towards the house.

"We've gotta move now," Guzman said as he glanced at the rest of the men. "This is what we've always trained for. Move quickly and shoot even quicker. We're obviously not going to be able to communicate with our two-way radios, so if we get split up, get off the property, turn your cell phones on, and we'll meet up after that." With that, Guzman stuck his right hand out and shook everyone's hand. "And, thanks for all you guys have done for me; I'm indebted to every one of you because of your selfless acts to help me during the past few months."

They finished their impromptu meeting and then left the surveillance room. Guzman left the room and returned with a can of gasoline. He pulled the small garbage can and a few chairs into the corner of the room. He poured a small amount of gasoline onto the chairs and walls before placing the gas can on the ground. He pulled out a lighter and tossed it into the garbage can. A small whooshing sound could be heard and the contents in the corner of the room turned into a raging inferno. Guzman exited the room and kept the door open to allow for oxygen to keep feeding the fire.

The rest of the group had armed themselves with several guns that were stored in a closet in the hallway. Sam reached into the closet and flipped a hidden switch; a faint whirring sound could be heard and a portion of the far wall began to slide to the side. Once the wall was open big enough for someone to squeeze through, Sam turned the switch off. None of them said a word as they bent over and entered into the darkness on the other side of the secret doorway. Once they were all inside the cramped passageway, Sam pressed another switch hidden in the mortar, and the secret door closed behind them.

Chapter 28

The first sign of trouble occurred as the armed officers continued toward the main buildings on the property. The signal was given for everyone to move forward, and then in an instant, the officers' portable radio communication was cut off.

What ensued after the communications failure was nothing short of utter chaos. Some officers stopped in their tracks, analyzing their options of either continuing without any means of communicating, therefore risking everyone's safety, or aborting the operation. The remaining officer's were committed one hundred percent and continued moving forward toward the main buildings on the property. These separate but distinct actions split up the advancing group of officers and severely diminished their ability to safely approach the main house.

The operations commander back at the Riverside County Sheriff's Office immediately realized that there was some sort of problem at the property. He ordered the USMSs two helicopters to respond to the property and provide air support for the advancing officers. These helicopters would be able to communicate with the containment team to let them know where any potential problems presented themselves. They could also get some eyes on the area around the house to see what the status of the advancing teams was.

Within five minutes, the first wave of heavily armed officers had tactically surrounded the house. The commander in charge of this group ordered an immediate siege of the house, since their search warrant didn't mandate that they knock before entering. Simultaneously, four flash bangs were thrown through a window on each side of the house. The percussion blasts from the flash bangs were sure to disorient anyone inside the house. Several smoke grenades were then tossed through the now broken glass windows, and dark colored smoke began drifting out of the windows.

Then the lead officer used a battering ram, and with two swift blows, knocked the door from its hinges. The remaining officers filed into the residence in an orderly fashion. Each officer had an assault rifles at the ready position and began quickly scanning the rooms to make sure they were clear of any occupants.

As the first floor was cleared of any suspects, heavy smoke began billowing out of the HVAC vents in the walls. The team commander quickly assessed the situation and determined that a fire was present in the basement. Not wanting to subject his officers to the possibility of the floor collapsing, the commander wisely decided to have the officers tactically retreat, so he could reassess the situation.

The officers exited the house just as quickly as they had arrived. Another officer came running up to the house just as the entry team exited the house.

"These barns are empty, and there aren't any signs of these guys," he said as he paused to catch his breath. "We still can't communicate with anyone through our radios."

"Our only option is to set up a perimeter around the house and call the fire department out here." The commander who had just exited the house yelled to the rest of the officers. "I'm sure these ass-holes planned to burn down their own house, and now we'll be blamed for causing another Ruby Ridge."

The officers followed their commander's directions and tactically retreated to set up the perimeter around the main housing area. Once the perimeter was set up, a group of four officers were designated to return to the river so they could try and communicate via their portable radios to the command post back at the sheriff's office.

∽∽

Meanwhile, Sam and his crew continued crawling down the cramped passageway as the dogs followed closely behind them. The original plan for the passageway called for enough room to stand up, but as the project had continued on, it became more apparent that it would be much easier to allow for enough room for someone to crawl down it. The entire length of the passageway spanned over several hundred feet to the east of the house.

As they neared the end of the passageway, Sam slid the small doorway to the side and slowly peered outside. The sun was still well below the horizon to the east and darkness was blanketing the entire area. Sam pulled out a pair of night-vision goggles and scanned the immediate area. He didn't notice any officers in the area and he motioned for the remaining guys to follow him out of the door.

The night was completely silent as they slowly made their way to the bank of the river, which was only ten feet from the hidden doorway. Once they reached the Birch River, Sam looked around and located one of the boats originally used by the advancing police officers. Their original plan was to wade down the river, but staying dry and taking off in one of the boats seemed like a better option.

Sam stayed on shore and kept the boat from floating away as the remaining guys quietly climbed inside. There was enough room for everyone to sit two to a bench. The dogs jumped into the boat and stood on the floor.

As Sam was placing his first foot into the boat, he heard noises approaching from the west. In his haste to get his second foot into the boat, Sam tumbled forward and fell into the gently flowing river.

Immediately, several flashlights from the advancing police officers clicked on and swept the area as they advanced towards the river.

Sam stood up in the river and scrambled to get back into the boat. He pulled himself over the side, and the rest of the men frantically paddled to pull away from the banks of the river.

They could hear excited voices coming from the banks as they disappeared into the darkness.

※

The four officers had almost made it to the river when they heard the loud splash. They turned on their flashlights and quickly advanced towards where the sound had originated. The rear officer tried his portable radio and still wasn't able to communicate with anyone.

The group reached the bank of the river and weren't able to see anything in the area. They continued searching the area and noticed that one of the boats was missing. They had no way of knowing if another group of officers were sent to try to communicate with the command post, or if it was the suspects who had taken the boat.

Just then, the distinct noise from the Bell helicopters could be heard approaching from the south. The helicopters conducted a flyby and then circled back and hovered high above the property. Each of the helicopters was equipped with thermal imaging cameras and would be able to pick up any movement from over a mile away.

The four officers decided to get into one of the boats and travel up the river to try to get enough reception on their portable radios so they could contact the command center. They all climbed into one of the boats and started the small electric motor. One of the officers pushed the boat away from the bank of the river, and they headed north.

Once they had traveled a hundred yards, their portable radios started working. After a minute of listening to other radio traffic, one of the officers on the boat was able to make contact with the command post. He updated the commanders on the status at the property and how all means of electronic communication was being scrambled. He let the command post know that they had to travel a hundred yards upstream from their drop off location to make contact with them.

"We've got a second boat traveling north on the Birch River," one of the helicopter pilots said over the portable radios. "It looks like there are several people riding in the boat. We'll keep them in our sights until some ground units can respond to the area and determine who's on this second boat."

Blake and Sergeant McGuire were positioned to the north of the property and heard the description of the boat traveling north on the river. Using guidance from the helicopter, they maneuvered closer to the fleeing boat. Most of the containment team decided to stay in their locations until it could be confirmed that these were the fleeing suspects. A few other officers who were in the immediate area called on their portable radios to let everyone know that they would be making their way towards the second boat as well.

Blake and Sergeant McGuire slipped onto the banks of the river just south of where the boats were originally deployed. Blake lay down behind a large oak tree and waited for the boat to approach from the south. Sergeant McGuire posted himself behind a large boulder twenty yards north of Blake. They both kept their assault rifles trained towards the river. Their night-vision goggles were in place, and they would have a distinct advantage over the suspects, who were most likely traveling by moonlight.

As Blake continued listening to the updates from the helicopters, he heard the sound of a boat making its way slowly up the river. Then a faint silhouette of the boat appeared around the slight bend in the river. Blake could see some movement in the boat, but couldn't make out how many people were inside.

Terror from Within

The boat continued towards them and slid slowly past Blake. When the boat was right in the middle of them, Blake made the decision to confront the subjects in the boat.

"Sheriff's office; stop the boat now," Blake yelled towards the boat as he pressed the button on his portable radio to transmit his actions.

Instantly, the helicopters turned on their bright spotlights and aimed them directly at the fleeing boat.

Sergeant McGuire and Blake stared in disbelief, as the boat was occupied by three vicious-looking dogs.

"What the hell is this?" Blake yelled in the direction of Sergeant McGuire as he stood up and stepped away from the large oak tree.

"I'm not exactly sure. Sam and his crew must have jumped out of the boat farther down the river," Sergeant McGuire said, also standing up to sit on the rock he had been using as cover.

Just then, a bright flash of light came from the direction of the boat and Blake felt a burning sensation in his right leg. It took him a split second to realize that he had been shot in the leg.

"Shots fired. Shots fired," Blake yelled frantically into his portable radio.

Blake and Sergeant McGuire scrambled back behind their cover as the boat continued moving slowly up the river.

A barrage of bullets continued flying over Blake and Sergeant McGuire's heads as they lowered themselves closer to the ground. Blake could hear voices over his portable radio, but he ignored them and tried to focus on the boat. He was sure that the entire cavalry was en route to provide back up.

Blake ignored the burning sensation in his leg and tried to focus on his front sight. His fine and complex motor skills were starting to diminish as he fumbled to keep his right pointer finger steady on the trigger of his AR-15.

They still weren't sure how many people were in the boat because they couldn't look out from behind their positions of cover without risking getting shot in the head.

Blake stayed low to the ground and moved to his left to find another position of cover. He needed to change positions to keep the shooters guessing on where he was. He set up behind another large tree and peered out from behind it to get a look at the boat. Blake focused his semi-automatic AR-15 at the middle of the boat and squeezed the trigger. The .223 round flew through the air and penetrated through the side of the boat. He continued pulling the trigger and riddled the boat with bullets. Blake was so focused on stopping the threat that he didn't hear Sergeant McGuire until he tapped him on the shoulder.

"Blake, that's enough. He's done. You don't need to shoot the boat to pieces," Sergeant McGuire yelled so Blake could hear him through his ringing ears.

Blake stood up and glanced back at the boat. Sergeant McGuire was right; the lone suspect was lying face down at the bottom of the boat. The three dogs were lying dead as well. Blake felt a momentary sense of sadness as he realized that the dogs happened to be in the wrong place at the wrong time.

Terror from Within

"Command from Sergeant McGuire; the threat in the boat has been stopped," Sergeant McGuire said calmly into his radio.

By now, the boat had careened off its original course and has lodged itself into the bank about twenty-five yards upstream.

They both hurried along the bank of the river and kept their rifles aimed at the boat in case the suspect happened to get up. They arrived at the boat several seconds later and several bullet wounds to the suspect's head made it obvious that he was deceased. The entire bottom of the boat was covered in deep-red blood.

Blake reached forward and pulled the boat further up the bank of the river. He pulled on a pair of black rubber gloves and confirmed that the suspect was dead.

Sergeant McGuire also donned a pair of black rubber gloves and assisted Blake in rolling the suspect over. They both remembered him clearly from a previous intelligence briefing. Guzman had been able to use a cell phone while incarcerated inside of the Humble County Correctional Facility, which eventually led to his escape. It was ironic that he had caused a diversion to buy enough time for the rest of the crew to flee the area.

"Command from Sergeant McGuire."

"Go ahead sergeant," one of the commanders back at the Riverside County Sheriff's Office said over the portable radio.

"Guzman was alone in this boat with several dogs. We need to have the helicopters use their thermal imagers to look for the remainder of this crew."

"10-4; we'll have them take care of this right away."

"We're starting to scan the area right now," one of the helicopter pilots said into his headset.

Most of the containment team had now converged to Blake and Sergeant McGuire's location. While Blake filled them in on what had transpired, Garcia noticed that Blake had a large amount of blood soaked into his pants.

"You need to get that leg looked at. I'll stick around here with you until the paramedics can examine your leg," Garcia said.

With his adrenaline working in high gear, Blake had forgotten that he was shot in the leg.

"I'll be fine. I'll have it looked at after we track down these other guys."

As Blake finished telling everyone what had transpired with the boat, one of the helicopter pilots called in a status update.

"We haven't been able to locate any of the suspects fleeing the area; does anyone have an idea what they might have used to leave the area?"

There was a long silence before Sergeant McGuire called over the radio.

"We've spoken with the officers who traveled up the river behind the suspect's boat, and they didn't hear or see anything as they traveled up the river."

"Roger that; we'll continue scanning the area. If anything new turns up, please keep us posted."

"We will do that, sir," Sergeant McGuire said as he looked over the officers who were assembled before him.

Chapter 29

A Riverside County sheriff's deputy was situated on the north end of Route 127, running stationary radar. He always sat in this location because it backed up to a state forest area and the chances of someone stumbling upon him were slim to none. He had begun his shift at 10:00 p.m. the previous night, and by this time in the morning he was having a hard time staying awake. The area around his squad car was completely dark except for the glow of his laptop computer and the red numerals of the radar unit that was mounted to his dashboard.

The deputy had closed his eyes for several minutes when the tone from his radar unit caused him to open his eyes. He glanced at the radar unit and it read 89 mph. Since the speed limit on this stretch of roadway was 70 mph, the deputy rubbed his eyes and waited for the vehicle to pass him. Then he pulled the gear shifter into drive and pressed on the gas pedal as he pulled out of his hidden spot. The vehicle disappeared over the crest of the hill in front of him, and then the deputy turned on his headlights. He quickly accelerated and began gaining ground on the speeding vehicle.

When the deputy got within two car lengths of the SUV, he read the license plate out to the county dispatchers. He advised them that he would be stopping the vehicle on northbound Route 127. The deputy activated his emergency lights and clicked on his spotlight before aiming it at the speeding vehicle. The dark-colored SUV accelerated, and it became apparent that the vehicle wasn't going to slow down.

"County, from 454, this vehicle is failing to stop," the deputy said into his radio.

"What is the reason for the stop?" the dispatcher asked as part of their protocol.

"It's for speeding 89 mph on Route 127. There aren't any other cars in the area and the roadway is dry."

"454, what is your current speed?"

"We're staying steady at 105 and we're still northbound on 127."

"We'll see if MSP or the Otter Tail Sheriff's Office has a unit that can assist."

"10-4."

The deputy updated his dispatchers as he continued traveling north on Route 127 as they began to approach Interstate 75. The deputy knew that if the SUV continued with speeds over 100 mph, then it would certainly have a hard time negotiating the merge onto Interstate 75.

"County, are there any other units in the area?"

"454, MSP has a unit on Interstate 75 just south of 127. He'll join up with you once you reach the interstate."

"10-4; thank you."

The SUV sped up and was approaching 120 mph as the road began to curve to the right and merge onto Interstate 75.

Suddenly, the SUV veered to the left and onto the gravel shoulder. The driver overcorrected to the right,

Terror from Within

which caused the SUV to begin barrel rolling down the middle of the road. Pieces of the vehicle were thrown in every direction as it continued rolling forward.

"County, this vehicle has rolled over. We're going to need rescue sent out to Interstate 75, just north of the 127 merger."

"10-4, 454; an ambulance will be en route to your location."

The SUV came to rest on its roof on the east side of Interstate 75. The deputy pulled up behind the SUV and aimed his spotlight at the car. The MSP trooper pulled his squad car right behind the deputy. The officers exited their cars and cautiously approached the SUV.

A loud popping noise came from inside of the SUV. This noise was followed by several more loud pops.

The officers pulled out their guns and scrambled behind the deputy's car to take cover.

"County, we've got shots fired from inside of this SUV," the deputy said after he pressed the button on his portable radio.

"10-4; we'll send some more units and have the ambulance stage south of your location."

The officer waited several minutes and didn't hear or see any movement from inside of the SUV.

Two Otter Tail sheriff's deputies arrived on scene for back up and parked their squad cars in front of the River side County squad car.

They jumped out of their cars and took cover behind the engine block.

The Riverside County deputy used the PA system from inside of his car and tried to make contact with someone inside of the SUV. After not receiving a response, all four of the officers decided to tactically approach the vehicle.

The Riverside County deputy's heart sank into his stomach as he took a look into the SUV. He immediately recognized Sam Jenson's face in the intelligence bulletin from the raid that was going to be conducted on the property of the suspects from the attack on the Humble County Sheriff's Office. All four suspects were dead from self-inflicted gunshot wounds.

"County from 454," the deputy said, trying not to sound too excited.

"454, go ahead."

"If you could please let the commanders at the sheriff's office know, we've got four suspects from their raid who are deceased at our location."

"10-4. I'm sure they'll appreciate the information."

Made in the USA
Lexington, KY
17 July 2011